The Ghost in the Book Shop

A Haunted hotel Mystery

Bonnie Elizabeth

My Big Fat Orange Cat Publishing

The Ghost in the Book Shop
My Big Fat Orange Cat
Mystery 2026

My Big Fat Orange Cat Publishing
MyBigFatOrangeCat.com

ISBN: 978-1-953363-27-5

Chapter One

That afternoon I went into Glade Springs to visit the Cornered Reader before my jiu jitsu class. The Cornered Reader was the little bookstore in the township that the resort I manage is nominally a part of. I say nominally because it's a drive over to town, a small and secluded place about thirty minutes or so from the larger town of Boone in the mountains of North Carolina.

The bookstore sits on a corner, which is probably where the name came from when Bill Richmond founded it. Bill has long since passed on and his nephew Clay now runs the place. It's a fun shop and draws tourists who come to the resort for rest and relaxation. The wood floors creak and groan, which my guests love. I mean I advertise as a haunted hotel, so creaks and groans are a big seller, though the hotel doesn't have many of those. Even better, the Cornered Reader is also haunted.

Clay's creaking floorboards and the slight squeal of the door offer spookiness the relative modernity of the hotel doesn't. The dim lighting in the loft where the used books reside is also a draw. Not to mention the skeleton that Clay has sitting up there in a corner reading a book on a rather dusty old brown and green overstuffed chair that might have existed nicely in my grandmother's house.

The place smells of books and dust and that indefinable something that starts to inhabit wood that's grown old and cranky with age. While the shelves were modern and bright with white paint covering the wood, and the aisles wide, the building itself did everything it could to show its age no matter what Clay did.

The fact that his Uncle Bill, now deceased, was often seen watching people from the front window in one of the pale blue club chairs suggested that Clay wasn't going to ever manage to make the place completely ordinary. Not so long as it was a bookstore at least, though Clay had no desire to change that.

He kept as much stock as he did because he often sold hard to find books online, along with the more popular titles. The old-fashioned signage out front and the talks that took place were very popular, which kept the place in the black. Around Halloween, Clay had various historical experts talk about the haunted history of this part of Appalachia.

He also had the occasional author come in and chat. Back in January my hotel had a cozy mystery writer's conference at the hotel, which had ended up being a disaster. We'd gotten snowed in and someone had been murdered. Clay had planned to come out and talk to them to see who could speak at the bookstore but, unfortunately, he'd been unable to get to us. By the time the roads were clear, the authors were more than ready to head home, most to warmer climates.

Today, he was attempting to get me to speak there. Or at least sign books. I'm not a writer, however, Olive, the former manager, was. Suzanne, one of my desk workers, was her editor and typist. Olive doesn't type. She's a ghost. She's also one of my best friends, even if she does take liberties, like insisting I be the public face of her author persona, as she called it. She avoided the term ghost writer because of the puns.

"I think Suzanne should be there as well," I said. Clay was behind the white desk that held a handful of books and a variety of small craft items that were made locally by a lovely woman named Shelly. She had asked if we could carry them in our little shop that catered to guests who had forgotten something or got a craving for snack foods but there wasn't much room. We did have a single rack of earrings near the cash register and, considering I thought they were over-priced, they were reasonable sellers. Paige, down in the spa, also carried a few of her earrings.

"She's just the editor," Clay pressed. "You came up with this stuff."

While everyone could see Olive—it's not like I have some gift that allows me to see ghosts—not everyone accepted that she was still there. It was hard to believe that a woman who managed a hotel would come back to haunt said hotel and continue to attempt to micro-manage everyone under her. But that was Olive. Dedicated to her job even in the ever after.

That would not be me. I hoped. I mean, how horrible would that be to feel as if one had to work even after death? I planned on resting, but hopefully not until after retirement with my cats and a few good police procedurals.

I had read Olive's books, which were cozy mysteries, but they weren't quite my cup of tea. I could talk about what happened but not why it was there. I might have the face of the author— Olive had had Suzanne take a photo and put on the author page on the various websites that sold books—but I was not the imagination behind the tales. I just wasn't up to it.

"Stop being shy. I've never known you to be shy," Clay said.

I wasn't. I often came into the bookstore and picked up something for myself or as a gift for someone. I'd been in a lot more lately as I'd worked on becoming more friendly rather than keeping to myself with my cats. While I could chat with anyone about light things, I was unfortunately rather poor at friendships and keeping up closer relationships.

"I'm not being shy. I just think that Suzanne had so much input, doing so much typing and editing that she'd be a good person to speak as well," I said. "I suppose I could sign the books for you."

Olive had asked me to do that when books needed autographing. I hated it. Hated signing Olive's name, which was not mine. In fact, once I'd nearly slipped and signed my own name. The story she'd given me to memorize was that I was using her name as a pen name as a sort of a tribute to her.

Clay agreed and pulled out a rather large stack of paperbound books. I knew that Suzanne sold them to bookstores and I figured that Clay would order a couple but this was more than a few. This could take me a bit to sign. I looked up at the clock. I'd come in to do a bit of shopping and perhaps chat with Bill if he were around, which he appreciated as so many people ignored him, but now I'd be signing books before my martial arts class.

I was nearly through the books when a woman came in heading towards the counter where I stood. Her graying hair was pulled up on her head with tendrils falling around her rather round face. Large sunglasses kept me from seeing her eyes. She wore a green cardigan over a white turtleneck sweater, though the seasons hadn't changed that far into winter. Her dark green slacks were nicely pressed.

Closing the second to the last book, I pulled the next one to me and signed Olive's name in the flourish I'd decided to use.

The woman's heels clicked on the creaky floors as she walked over to me. I thought I heard Bill say uh oh.

"Can I help you?" Clay asked. He was gathering up the signed books and putting them on a cart so he could take them back out to the display table. He had a sign that advertised autographed copies.

The woman looked at the book and at my signature.

"How dare you steal my cousin's name!" she shouted at me.

My jaw must have dropped far enough that if Olive had been here, she'd accuse me of catching flies.

"Olive was my beloved cousin! How dare you use her name to sell books! I read about you. You work where she used to work so you can't say it's just coincidence. Do you have no care for the people who loved her that she left behind?"

Taken aback, I stepped away, not certain what to say. Lots of things crossed my mind such as the fact that Olive was my best friend and she'd never mentioned family. She certainly hadn't mentioned a cousin that would think of her as beloved. I'd also been at her funeral which had been mostly people who were local to the area. Of course, that had been nearly thirty years ago so it wasn't impossible I had missed someone.

Of course, I and Ari Bowman, one of the owners, had taken the seats reserved for primary mourners. It seemed poor form to bring that up when this woman was obviously distraught about something.

"I'll be suing!" she cried. "You'll not make a fortune off my poor, dear cousin's memory!"

And with that she walked back out, leaving Clay and I staring after her.

Bill snorted in his chair. "Idiot," he muttered loud enough for us to hear.

I hoped he was talking about the stranger and not me.

Chapter Two

Clay ran a hand through his hair and then shook his head. An upbeat song, a pop song popular in the 80s, played in the background. It was the sort of song that made you want to dance, or perhaps that was just me having spent my dancing days listening to such music. Still, it was a jarring contrast to the recent encounter, though it played on low volume.

I cleared my throat and handed him back the last book in the pile I'd signed.

"I don't quite know what to say," he began. His hands shook a bit as he placed it on the pile and then he shook himself. You'd think the stranger had accused him of a crime rather than me.

"I suppose if she does actually try and sue, I'll have to get an attorney. I'm not sure what grounds she has, though," I said. This was particularly true since she hadn't been at the funeral. "I don't recall her from Olive's memorial service, though that was years ago. Still, it was left up to Ari to plan things."

"I was a bit young to know Olive," Clay said. "She came in sometimes when my uncle was here."

"Ayup," Bill said from the chair. I had a feeling he was dying to interject his opinion on things.

Clay ignored him. I wanted to ask if he didn't see Bill, but I knew he did. Sometimes when no one else was around, Clay would be sitting in a chair and talking to him. And, as I said, there's nothing special about my ability to see ghosts, but perhaps there is something special about the fact that I was willing to listen to them.

"I think my uncle said she would sometimes be half drunk and he worried about her driving all the way out to the Neary-Ten."

The resort was called the Neary-Ten because we were nearly to the Tennessee border. At one time it had been the Quiet Glade Hotel but when the Bowmans purchased it, they hadn't liked the name. Or so I was told. I came in long after they'd purchased it. The generation Olive and I worked with had inherited the thing as a sort of white elephant in their portfolio. But they liked it enough to keep it, which was a relief, usually.

"I do recall hearing about that," I said. In fact, it had been something I'd looked into a few months ago when we'd finally solved the mystery of the ghost in room 785. It seemed he only showed up on the day he died. Fortunately, the guest in the room this time had called down immediately when he'd appeared. I suspect, given that she'd been married to the man in life, that his spirit had stuck around a little longer than usual.

But at any rate, Olive had been worried she'd killed him. Later we found out he had probably run off the road avoiding a deer in a single car accident. On the one hand, Olive was relieved that she hadn't accidentally killed someone in a car wreck. On the other, she was disappointed that she wasn't what she termed a "badass murderer" who had gotten away with it.

There are pluses and minuses to everything, I suppose.

"It's too bad that her family didn't bother to be there for her. I didn't think they were from around here," Clay went on.

"I haven't ever heard her talk about anyone," I said. I hoped that if Clay heard the present tense, he knew that Olive still wandered around the resort.

He just nodded.

"Well, I need to get going." I picked up my purse and waved at him. I gave Bill a nod. He grinned at me and went back to watching the people walking around the downtown area.

The day was getting on, the sun just barely peeking over the mountains leaving the sky streaked in purples and pinks. A car honked down the way. I turned but didn't notice who it was. Three women passed me going the other direction, laughing. They all carried bags of items. I figured they were heading down to Carmichael's, which was one of the family restaurants in town. It was a popular place for people to celebrate birthdays and anniversaries if they didn't want to drive out to the Neary-Ten or all the way over to Boone.

While I could have wished for the town's patronage as far as keeping my workers busy, I had to admit, if they were going to be drinking, it was probably safer in town than out by us. While you could always call for a car, that still required a certain amount of planning, not to mention the fact that calling for a car would incur a further cost.

I knew that not everyone was willing to pay the extra. And that people had a tendency to overestimate their abilities when impaired. It was a training all our bar staff went through at least once a year and I'd sat in on more than one occasion. I firmly believed I ought to know the ins and outs of all hotel positions.

I walked around the corner. Behind the bookstore was a large parking lot with the local grocer at the far end. Across the street was the dojo. It was a low building of painted black brick and black wood trim. The door itself was bright red. The colors gave the simple square box more of an Asian feel but it looked a bit out of place in the hodge-podge of Glade Springs.

My car was in the lot along with three other cars, including one that belonged to Dori, one of the cooks at the Neary-Ten's steak house. Dori was a martial arts student and teacher. She taught the class after mine. Hers was a more advanced class than the beginner jiu jitsu I practiced.

Brett, the owner, and Alyssa, his receptionist, parked down the hill around the back. The building was on a slope and the downstairs walked out to the back parking area. Brett was actively working to remodel the building so he could make more use of the space downstairs. Right now, it was just storage and staff rooms which never got used because classes were upstairs.

I walked in and waved at Alyssa. She gave me a big smile. She sat behind a reception desk that was the same black as the outside of the building, though the desk's paint had endured quite a few more scratches. It was in sharp contrast to the pale wood floor and the stark white walls that had the sort of sheen one gets in a bathroom.

Overhead, the old florescent lights gave off a low hum that could be heard over the tinkle of the fountain that sat in the corner of the entry area. To my right were the women's locker rooms and to the left were the men's. Next to the desk was the door back into the main gym area where we met.

"Brett will announce this in class, but he wants me to tell everyone as well," she said, leaning forward eager to impart information.

I paused on my way to the women's locker room to put away my stuff and change clothes for the class.

"Today will be the last class. They're going to start demolition on this building tomorrow," She paused, waiting to see how I took that information.

"I had heard it wouldn't happen until after the first of the year," I said. It didn't bother me. I liked my jiu jitsu classes, but I wasn't married to them. I'd started with self-defense and worked into jiu jitsu. They got me out of the house at least one night a week and I'd begun to meet people in town. They forced me to get out of my rut in the hotel with my cats and my apartment and be more friendly. It had hit home to me this past year that I needed to get out more and make human connections.

While I wasn't likely ever to be the most popular person, nor did I want to be, I was learning to share nice chats and find people that I felt I could count on. Vulnerability and the sort of intimate friendships some people had still eluded me, but I could no longer say my only real friends were my cats, my sister, who lived across the country, and a ghost.

"The inspector came in to get a sense of what was going to be done and what could be salvaged but there are tons of structural issues. I guess the plumbing is bad and has been leaking downstairs and causing problems with some of the weight bearing walls. He really wanted us to close today, but Brett ignored him. He wants to be here so he can tell everyone. No need to change because there's no class. Just the announcement and he'll have more details."

"That's terrible," I said. It was also terrible that Brett was making Alyssa sit at a desk in a building that the building inspector wanted to close. I walked a bit more softly across the wood floor.

I started towards the locker room.

"You can't go in there!" Alyssa called. "Plumbing issue, remember?"

"Shoes?" I asked. I knew we weren't supposed to talk on the gym floor in street shoes. The mats that were usually down were missing. In fact, the items that normally hung on the walls were all gone.

"Take them off and leave them by the door," Alyssa told me. I saw a couple of other pairs.

Inside the gym, the shiny floor was unfamiliar to me considering it had always been covered in thick black mats. I saw two large men carrying out a couple of mats that had been moved to the side of the gym. They headed through a back door I didn't know existed.

"Maggie," Brett said, coming over. "Have a seat on the floor. Sorry about not having mats but we're hurrying to get things out. I'll be pulling everything else that we can get out overnight. They start demolition tomorrow."

A couple of other women sat on the floor and two men. They were all sitting and waiting as if we were actually going to have class rather than just waiting on an announcement.

As other people arrived, Brett went through the same speech he'd given to me. When everyone regularly in class had arrived, he sighed.

"I have no idea how long we'll be out for. All payments for next month will be stopped. You won't have to do anything. I'll be taking care of any issues that pop up around that. Next month I hope to have a better idea of how long the new building will take. I guess that there was a huge plumbing issue that ruined a lot of the wood on the lower level. The estimates I got earlier today suggest that tearing the place down and starting again is the way to go."

"How will you get on?" someone asked.

"I have online courses for people to do at home," Brett said. "I'm looking into a couple of rental places, which is why I'm only planning on closing for a month."

"Oh good," one of the students said. "I'd hate to miss class for a long time. I'd get out of shape."

"We'll all be getting back into shape when we return," Brett said. He gave us a list of things he wanted us to do at home. I couldn't imagine how my two Siamese cats would take to me going through all those motions when I was in our living room. It wasn't a large space by any means.

He talked for a bit longer. Others had questions, some about how often to do our home exercises. Brett had always given us things to practice, which I tried to run through at least once, but these exercises were more intense than usual. He was clearly torn about wanting to show us but being mindful of the fact that the building had to come down. Of course, if it had been going to fall apart, one would have thought it would have done so while we were all jumping around in the gym doing our work and not that evening when one person demonstrated the moves.

Finally, the questions subsided. We all got up and went out to the front to gather our shoes. Dori, my cook, was at the reception desk with Alyssa. She waved at me when she noticed I was there.

"I'll see you tomorrow?" I asked. Dori worked on Wednesdays and I usually went down to check in to see how things were going. As manager, I checked in with everyone at least once a week in person and was always available by email. I tried not to micromanage too much but I had no doubt there were times when I failed at that miserably.

"Hope so!" Dori said smiling.

I headed back to my car to go back to the resort. I completely forgot the extra clothing I stashed in my locker until I got back to my apartment. I had fed the cats and myself and was thinking about starting a load of laundry when I remembered. I worried for a few minutes thinking that I'd not be able to get it, but, surely, I could head back and grab something, especially if I got there before they'd removed everything.

Chapter Three

The drive back to town after dinner, when it was dark, was less enchanting than it had been in the afternoon. During the afternoon, in the fall, the colorful leaves kept me company. There was always a new rainbow of oranges, golds, and greens to see and enjoy. Because even on the main highway there wasn't a lot of traffic, I was able to enjoy the colors and feel part of something. The other cars around me reminded me I was part of civilization all the way into town.

Once in Glade Springs, while there might not be many cars, someone was always parked along the street. People strolled from shop to shop, sometimes browsing. I was never quite alone.

At night, the streets felt more deserted and the lights too dim. I didn't mind driving back home, knowing that I'd settle into the apartment I had at the hotel. But going into town, the emptiness bothered me, as if I feared I'd get there and the place would be destroyed. My imagination was a bit wild.

I rarely went into town after about six. I'd share the road

with other cars whose owners had been out seeing the sights and returning to civilization. In the other direction cars heading out to the hotel for dinner or perhaps to check into a room would zoom by.

But tonight, my drive took place later. It wasn't that there wasn't any traffic, just that there was less than usual. Add to that a new moon and the night seemed particularly dark.

In town, the shops were either closing or had already done so. Bright lights from the bar a few blocks up shone, along with some lights from Carmichael's further down. Other than that, there were merely evening lights, the bright signs gone dark and I saw only one person on the street. Even Bill didn't appear to be in the front window of the bookstore, having faded out to wherever ghosts faded out to, or perhaps watching out the upper window on the side of the building.

I parked around the corner at the dojo. I smelled something like burnt tires. I would have liked to check to see if there was something on mine, but it was far too dark. There were a handful of emergency lights around the dojo but it didn't appear that any of the workers who were supposed to be removing stuff were around.

Looking around the corner before heading to the door, I spotted a truck. Perhaps Brett had gotten only a few men or perhaps the others had gone out to eat dinner. It was a bit late, but if they'd been working, perhaps they were eating just now.

Heart sinking that I'd lost the sweats that I had left, I tried the door. It was unlocked. The lights inside were low, giving the dark wood desk an eerie feel. I crossed to the locker room, the one Alyssa wouldn't let me go into earlier. I should have thought to ask about my clothing then.

The door opened to a short hall to my right and I went down that to get to the large room where the lockers had been lined in neat rows with benches across for changing. Now, the lockers and benches were gone. The room was just a huge empty space except for a bundle of clothing in the far corner. The light was too dim to make it out.

I walked over there, intending to pick out the stuff that was mine, grateful that I wasn't the only one that had forgotten to remove clothing. When I got there, I bent to pick through the pile, only to realize that it was a body.

"Are you okay?" I called out loudly, remembering something about talking to someone in my first aid training. I shook them a little but their arm just flopped over to the front from where it lay on their side. Bringing my phone around for more light, I saw that the person was a man, someone I didn't recognize. He had to have been a worker.

He was curled on his side. His hand had been resting on his hip but now it lay awkwardly on the floor. Reaching out to check and see if I could find a pulse in his neck, I had a feeling I wasn't going to find one.

Distantly, I heard the front door close, an odd sound without the jangle of the bell Brett had on it. I jumped and turned around, wondering who else was coming in. I dialed 9 1 1, not bothering with the pulse. I needed help.

No one entered the women's locker room, nor did they call out. Even while I spoke into the phone, telling the operator that I had found a man who might be dead on the floor of the mostly empty dojo, no one came to see what was going on. I wasn't being quiet. I knew that it was possible to hear conversations between the reception area and the locker rooms. I'd heard people talking out front and people talking inside, even with music. It could only be more pronounced now.

A siren sounded. It quickly got closer to where I was. The 911 operator stayed on the phone with me. I looked around to the locker room door to see if I could find an actual light. Before turning it on, I realized that perhaps the police would want to see exactly what I had found.

When the door banged open again and a uniformed office came in, I hung up the phone. He checked on the man and then called for a detective, asking me to wait. He escorted me out to the car, leaving the man lying on the floor alone. My guess that the poor man on the floor was dead had been right on.

When the officer asked me what had happened, I babbled on about worrying about my sweats, which seemed so trivial now that there was a dead person in the dojo. Still, the officer wanted to know what I was doing there. I'd finished and the officer stood around by the front door after letting me climb into my car where it was warmer. The night air was chilly and I was already shivering from the shock I'd had.

In a few minutes a large dark sedan pulled up. From the way the officer's shoulders raised slightly in tension, I figured this must be the detective he'd called.

A small female figure got out, her head held high, though even that only brought her up to the uniformed officer's shoulder. I knew by the set of her shoulders and the height that it was Detective Alice Granger, Al to my friend Lyle, Detective Granger to me. In my mind, due to her size, I called her Detective Tinkerbell.

Granger went inside without looking around. The door made the faintest sound out in front. No one had come out of the building since I had left. Someone must have been leaving about the time I found the body. I shuddered, realizing that perhaps I had been in the building with the killer.

I stepped out of the car and looked down the hill. The truck that had been there earlier was gone. I hadn't heard a car but, of course, I'd been busy on the phone with the 911 operator. I went over to the police officer to tell him what I remembered. He made a note and asked me to go back to my car.

Granger spent a long time in the dojo. Another sedan pulled up and her less obnoxious partner, Detective Penn pulled up. Penn was about as non-descript as person could be and still breathe. Brown hair, medium height, average features. He was the sort of person who would make a great spy because no one would ever notice him wandering around. Even if they did, they probably couldn't have described him.

He spoke to the uniform for a few minutes. Then he, too, went inside.

Moments later Granger came out. She spoke to the uniform and marched purposefully over to my car. When she saw me, she gave me one of her trademark glares. Lyle assures me that it's just her way. I was equally certain that she hated me and was certain I was a murderer.

She'd been the detective when one of our cleaning people had found Floyd Bowman dead in the owner's suite. She'd interrogated me quite heavily because, as manager, I'd gone up to find out what was going on and had made the call. While Floyd was no one's friend, least of all mine, I hadn't murdered him.

It appeared that I was about to be grilled within an inch of my life once again.

Chapter Four

It was early morning before I got to drive back home. Not morning as in the time most people were getting up, but that time of the morning when most sensible people were asleep in their beds. At this hour, I was alone the entire drive. My headlights were the only ones along the curving dark road that brought me back to the hotel. I had a parking garage space below the restaurant that allowed me to walk through a long hallway, which, fortunately, was lighted, to where my apartment was.

I was cold, tired, and annoyed. It wasn't as if Detectives Granger and Penn didn't know where to find me. They knew I worked at the Neary-Ten. They knew I lived on the premises. They also knew I wasn't a flight risk. I didn't even know the dead man so I couldn't come up with a reason they might think I had murdered him.

Granger, however, had had me go over a dozen times why I'd come to the dojo at that time of night to get my stuff rather than waiting until the morning. I repeated my tale, sighing about the third time she'd quizzed me. Still, because

I had no idea who the person was, another thing she pressed me on several times, even warning me that she'd be back if she found a connection between us, she finally gave up.

Chai and Latte, my two Siamese were as annoyed with me as I was with Granger. They'd had their dinner but after dinner, they were most accustomed to getting some attention from me while I sat on the sofa and watched television. Even if I'm not home in the evening, I am typically back before this hour of the morning.

Both were in the bedroom and both leaped off the bed the minute I entered the room and hid beneath it, as if I were a complete stranger to them. It was probably good that I like my work and dislike travel. That may be an odd thing for a hotel manager to admit, but it was true. I prefer to hear about travels from other people.

The idea of packing a bag and gathering all the necessities I might need at my age, and then suffering either the neck aches of driving or the headaches of plane travel, did not appeal. There was nowhere I wanted to see badly enough to go.

When I was younger, I'd dreamed of visiting Scotland. My ex-husband had taken me there and we'd had a horrid time, fighting just about every minute. It was not something I wanted to repeat. Instead, I appreciated my quiet life with the cats, watching the occasional travel documentary and running the hotel.

From time to time, I was required to go somewhere for a conference, but the last few times I'd sent Mark, my day manager. He'd loved it. If such things came up and I could foist off the travel on him again, I'd do so.

At any rate, by the time I'd washed up and was ready to climb into the bed, the boys were back in their places, though the glares they gave me told me they were not pleased with me. When my alarm went off barely three hours later, I wasn't exactly pleased with me either.

I laid back down, trying to decide if I should get up or leave a message for Mark that I'd be in late. While I might be exhausted, my mind was too active to let me fall back to sleep. The shock of finding a body suddenly hit me, and I ended up crawling out of bed and making myself some toast and coffee.

Chai and Latte got their morning meal. They were friendlier when it appeared that our routine would be held to. Clearly their annoyance the night before was worrying that they might miss their breakfast, not that either of them had to worry much. Chai was rather plump, built a bit like a football rather than a sleek Siamese. Latte probably ate more than his brother but he remained rather lean.

Both had settled on the sofa, ready to begin their exciting day of bird watching out the living room window when I went out the door to head upstairs to the main lobby.

I planned to treat myself to fancy coffee from our coffee shop that morning. A group of people all dressed in black were milling around the basement in front of the main conference area. Urns of coffee and tea, the smell of which perked me up, were sitting on tables outside the conference room. We had a huge room downstairs and when the drapes were opened the view out over the forest we abutted was spectacular. Today, someone had draped the doors and the walls in black cloth and the tables had our classic black coverings. It felt funereal.

I had forgotten we had a conference. I seemed to recall there'd been a great deal of negotiation. The ghost hunters were coming for Halloween, which was only a week away so this group had had to pick another date. This was normally about peak leaf color time so our prices went up because our rooms were so popular.

The organizers hadn't been pleased. Our event coordinator had been pulling her hair out over the demands. And then she'd had to field the slight threats of not getting bitten when the conference goers came. This was a conference dedicated to all things vampire, including, it seemed, people who thought they were vampires. The conference title, Vampire Love, was not something that appealed to me in the least.

Still, I'd have to ask Olive if ghosts knew if vampires were real or if this was all make-believe.

No one stopped me as I went up the stairs to the lobby. After all the black down there, I was glad of the bright windows outside, even if the day was slightly overcast. We could be in for some rain.

"Morning," I said to Suzanne who was manning the desk. Mark would be in soon but Suzanne covered the short portion of the early morning when Addy, the night manager was gone, and Mark had yet to come in. I was usually only a phone call away. On those rare occasions when I wasn't, Mark or Addy would cover for me, although Suzanne was excellent at her job. We were lucky to have her.

"Morning," she said. "You look as if you didn't get any sleep."

"That bad?" I asked. I paused by the large brown front desk that went with the whole lobby esthetic. While the floor tiles were white and there were large windows to the front, the large stone fireplace made this look like the mountain resort that it was. Soft classic music played in the background. The lobby bar across the way was a dark cave. While it wasn't shuttered and people could sit inside, the lights were off and the walls were painted black in there, to create a cozier feel.

"I think the circles under your eyes are even with the tip of your nose," Suzanne said though she did say it with a smile.

"I'm off to get some more coffee and then maybe I can explain," I told her. I headed down to the café. A bright hallway led me there, the lights feeling like an insult to my sleep deprived brain. It wasn't quite a hangover, but I definitely wasn't ready for the day.

The hostess asked me if I needed a seat and I shook my head, giving her my order for the largest, strongest coffee we have. She wrote down my order and gave it to one of our to-go runners. I went over to sit on the bench to wait.

There were plenty of people still eating breakfast, most in black clothing. A few had on capes. While many of the conference attendees were downstairs, many were up here, under the bright lights. As far as I could tell, everyone seemed to be eating rather than drinking blood, not that we served blood or anything.

A woman came up, ordered a hot tea, and sat down beside me. She put her bag down at her feet and leaned back.

I didn't start talking to her. In the morning, some people, like myself, just want to be left alone. I stared straight ahead, thankful that it didn't take too long for them to return with my coffee. The runner even had the woman's tea at the same time. I appreciated the promptness of my employees and I thanked them.

I walked back to the front office. Suzanne was answering some questions for an elderly couple. They seemed concerned about the young people all in black. And the fact that the parking lot was nearly full. They didn't want to drive off to look at leaves and not have a space to come back to.

"We'll definitely have something," Suzanne assured them. "If there's an issue, you can use the valet parking. I'll make a note on your room that you should be comped for that. Is that okay?"

The couple seemed happy enough and I watched as they left the desk. I went into the closet that was my office and slumped down behind my oversized desk. I swear that thing was larger than my bed and took up most of the minimal amount of space that I had. The built in book-shelves that held records and odds and ends that I might need behind me didn't help, nor did the tiny table and two chairs. Whoever had originally designed this must have assumed that hotel managers could fly over these things and get down to work.

As I turned on my computer, sipping my coffee, I felt a chill on the back of my neck. As it was late in the year, the air conditioning wouldn't have come on. Olive had popped in behind me.

"Morning Olive," I said.

"You look tired," she said. "And you don't often get a coffee that large."

"I am." I admitted. I entered my password and waited for the computer to finish booting.

"Did you finally go on a date with Lyle?" Olive asked.

Lyle was a local park ranger. He often helped out if there was something wrong at the resort because we were on the edge of the national forest. He was a friend, but we were not romantically involved in any way. I doubted either of us wanted that. I certainly couldn't imagine the way my life might change if I gave in and started a relationship with him.

"Lyle and I are not at all romantically involved," I said.

"Oh pooh. You ought to be. It's clear that when you get yourself into one of your situations he becomes quite concerned," Olive said.

I didn't have the energy to glare at her, though she'd floated around to sit in one of the chairs next to the desk. I wasn't ever quite sure how she sat when she could walk through walls.

"We're perfectly fine being friends," I said. "One worries about their friends as well as romantic interests. You were worried enough about me to distract a woman long enough that help was able to arrive to save me."

At the first of the year, during a particularly bad snowstorm, I had nearly been murdered in my own apartment. Olive had assisted by popping in and distracting the woman so that Jake and Lyle had time to get down there and help me.

"Well, I didn't exactly want to have you haunting the hotel with me," Olive said. She fingered the pearls that she wore at her neck and then said, "Or worse, that you would die and not return."

The last was said a bit more quietly, which suggested Olive wasn't particularly keen on admitting such a thing. It made me feel good that she'd miss me. If I had a choice, there was no way I was sticking around the hotel after I died.

"But what did go on?" Olive demanded after a brief silence. The computer was ready for me to start work, but my brain was a bit less engaged. It was too bad I couldn't just turn it on the way you turned on a computer.

"I found out yesterday that the dojo is being torn down starting today. I guess there were some major plumbing issues and Brett either had to fix them or not use the building. Instead of the remodel he had hoped to do, he's doing a complete tear down. I'm surprised he was able to get someone in so quickly, but perhaps there's more that I don't know about. Anyway, I left and then realized I had sweats in the lockers there and wanted to go get them before the building was torn down. Brett made it sound like there would be people there all night."

"So far this doesn't explain why you're so tired. Glade Springs might be a drive but it's not like it's days away," Olive said. She watched me carefully.

"I'm getting there. When I pulled up, there was a truck in back but no lights. I tried the door and it was open. I went in. The lockers were gone but there was what I thought was a pile of clothing in the corner. It wasn't. It was a person and he was dead. I ended up having to stay there and get grilled by Detective Granger until the wee hours."

"It seems as if Tinkerbell has taken against you a bit, hasn't she?" Olive said. Olive was very aware of how much time Granger, nickname Tinkerbell, had spent grilling me about Floyd and my relationship, such as it was. Quite honestly, I'm not sure there was anyone who'd met Floyd who hadn't had a reason to want him dead. Instead, it had been one of my bartenders and I still felt that loss. He'd been a nice young man, or so I thought.

"She was actually a bit less rude this time. Of course I didn't know the man who died. I can't say that I've ever seen him before. Just my luck if it turns out he's stayed at the hotel or something."

I took a sip of my coffee, hoping that the caffeine would kick in. My gaze settled on Suzanne and the fact that she was talking to Detective Penn or else another equally nondescript man.

"Is it me, or is that Granger's partner, Detective Penn?" I asked.

Olive turned. "Oh dear. I suspect that you are not going to have a good day." And with that she popped out, making me wish I could do the same. I stood up to go out there, expecting that I'd have to explain how I didn't know that a guest in our hotel had been murdered in a dojo where I'd found the body.

Chapter Five

Penn stood behind the chest high reception desk, across from where Suzanne was typing on a computer. He looked as tired as I felt. He also held a large travel mug of delicious smelling coffee. I wondered how many he'd had.

He wore what I considered the Glade Springs detective uniform of dark jeans and a blazer over a shirt of some sort. Penn had put on a fresh one. Last night, he'd had a t-shirt on under the blazer. This morning it was a button down. His hair was more neatly combed as well. I wondered if he'd slept or just gotten a quick shower and some food.

"Ms. Davenport," Penn said when I appeared.

"How can we help you?" I asked.

"We've identified the dead man," Penn said. "He was working on the demolition. The foreman said that a man staying at your hotel had come into town to visit him and the dead man had arrived to work a little later because of it. We'd like to talk this man."

"The guest's name?" I asked.

"Rory Ingles," Suzanne said.

I looked over her shoulder and saw that Ingles had checked in yesterday afternoon. It would have been while I was talking to Clay at the bookstore, fortunately. Not that it mattered if I knew the man's friend or not. Still, the further I could keep myself from this mystery, the better. It appeared that Rory was here for the vampire conference.

"We can call up to the room, but I can't give out information on a guest," I said. "Not without a warrant. However, it appears that he may be here for the vampire conference going on downstairs. The organizer is a man named Logan Fulton and he may be able to tell you more."

Penn gave me a long look as if he weren't sure what to say.

"Our attorneys have been very clear that our policy is to protect guest's privacy," I babbled, hoping that he'd drop that stare and go on downstairs to the conference. It could be argued that I'd gone too far by suggesting that Rory was there for the conference. I knew he had because of the charge code on the room, however, I could just be guessing that he was part of the conference.

Suzanne waited quietly. She seemed far less uncomfortable with Penn's stare than I was. Of course, she hadn't found a dead body in an otherwise empty building.

"A vampire conference?" Penn finally repeated, the question clear in the way he said it.

"We have all sorts of conferences here," I said. "My event coordinator often knows more about them and the people than I do. I only know that there are a lot of folks walking around dressed in black today."

"These people all think they're vampires?" Penn couldn't seem to let go of that idea.

"I'm not sure if it's just people who think they're vampires or people who just like vampires—you know in books and movies and things," I hastened to add when Penn raised an eyebrow.

"Who knew?" Penn muttered and turned from the desk. He headed downstairs, clearly having familiarized himself with the hotel's layout. He'd probably done so during the last investigation on the premises. At least this time, the murder hadn't actually happened here, but in town.

"A body?" Suzanne asked. "And you didn't ask more about it."

Which meant I had to explain what had happened yesterday to her. Fortunately, the morning was quiet. Most of our guests were either downstairs or hurrying down there for the conference, so there were few questions for the desk. I had a feeling those would come midday.

When I was done, Suzanne shook her head. "You have the worst luck."

I had to agree.

"You'd think," I said after a moment, "that a vampire conference would have had more going on at night. I heard nothing from any of them when I came in this morning but plenty of people were wandering around first thing this morning."

"You would think," Suzanne agreed. "But perhaps because it didn't begin until today they're just getting an early start. Who knows what's going on later?"

While I agreed with the sentiment, I knew that somewhere in my notes, I could find out what was happening later. I went into my office to do just that.

Chapter Six

I sipped at my coffee and tried to concentrate on work. I had schedules to do and some reports to go over. I signed off on a large order that Susie, the event coordinator had scheduled for next week. She had warned me that was coming up. When she couldn't be around, I was often the point person on the events, but after the murder at the beginning of the year, I'd been trying to stay more hands off.

It was difficult for me to figure out why. I didn't really expect another murder, certainly not at a conference, but I just felt I wanted to leave the work of event coordinating in someone else's hands. It could also have been the fact that it happened when we were snowed in that made me feel claustrophobic whenever I thought about acting point for a conference.

Lost in my thoughts I was only passingly aware of the smell of French fries reaching my nose, reminding me that the bar had opened and the music was playing a popular tune from about 1982. The fact that I could name the year made me feel old.

I stood up and stretched. I stepped out to the desk.

Mark was there but Suzanne had taken off, probably to lunch.

"How are things?" I asked.

"Surprisingly quiet," Mark said. "The vampire group doesn't seem to have a lot of questions. Either that or they're waiting until tonight."

He chuckled at his own joke.

"Suzanne said there was an elderly couple asking about all the people in the black," I told him. "We could get a few more of those. Let me know if it seems to be a problem. It is rather odd to have a bunch of young people in black side by side with the leaf watchers."

"I think they're called leaf peepers," Mark said not looking at me. He seemed interested in something on the computer.

"What is it?" I asked.

"I thought I looked yesterday and we were supposed to be full today, but we've got three open rooms."

"Things happen," I said. "It's why we have last minute rates."

"It's weird. I'm sure I checked in the person in 336 for the conference. It has the conference rate, but they've already left."

"Maybe the conference wasn't for them?" I suggested.

"The check out time was midnight last night," Mark replied. "Seems like they'd have waited until the actual start of the conference."

"Wasn't there an informal meet and greet downstairs?"

"Yeah, but it seems odd to me. They came all the way from Nevada to stay here. I'd have spent the night. I mean, they paid for it and it's not like getting to the airport in the middle of the night would change anything."

"That is odd," I said. "Name?"

"Nancy Ingles," he said.

"Interesting. Penn was here earlier asking about a Rory Ingles."

"The detective?" Mark looked surprised. I couldn't believe Suzanne didn't tell him but it appeared she hadn't. It was up to me to tell him about my evening and the body I had found.

Mark shook his head. "Just wild."

"Wild is right."

"Penn seems like a good guy. When he was starting out, he arrested my sister a couple of times for petty theft and drunk and disorderly. He's always been known as a hard ass, but he was kind to her, or at least kinder than some of the others."

"He strikes me as someone who's hard to read," I said. "I mean, I bet he's pleasant to everyone when he can be. It's one of the many things that keeps him from being noticed."

"True. I think that's why Alice Granger got promoted before him, although she was several years his junior on the force. She was always a tough one. She was always on my cousin Barlow about vandalism largely because she'd caught him once when he was a teen. He's grown out of it, not that he's exactly on the straight and narrow, but he isn't defacing property. But when she was in uniform, if someone complained, she'd show up at his house or accost Barlow somewhere asking him what he was doing when the vandalism happened. Ironically, he'd never been into tagging. He was caught for keying cars downtown, but she acted like any sort of defacement was him."

"I had no idea," I said. I had learned that Mark's family wasn't exactly law abiding but he'd never talked about them in terms of our detectives.

Mark shrugged. "Just interesting to me. I wonder if Penn got to run this one."

"He probably got stuck driving out here because Granger didn't want to." I thought about telling Mark how I called her Detective Tinkerbell in my mind, but then thought better of it. The only place that nickname belonged was in my head. I'd hate for her to overhear it and then really dislike me. Bad enough that I'd shared the nickname with Olive, though she would have taken credit for the name should Granger dislike it. The detective hadn't exactly endeared herself to Olive when I'd nearly been killed by the person who had murdered Floyd. Granger hadn't even come to investigate the incident.

A middle-aged woman in baggy jeans and a light sweater came over to the desk. She'd come over from the bar area, glancing at the fire in the large fireplace we had in the middle of the lobby before walking towards us. I stepped back lest she be worried about interrupting. It was probably a good call because as soon as I did so, she hurried over.

I slipped back into my office.

My ears perked up when she asked about Nancy Ingles. She said she was supposed to meet her there that evening but couldn't get a hold of her. She was aware that Nancy had checked in last night, but hadn't heard from her at all that day.

"I just came in from town because I wasn't really interested in her vampire lovers conference," the woman said.

Mark swallowed. I could almost hear what he was thinking.

"I don't have anyone currently listed in our computer by that name," he said.

I tapped out a note to Lyle. I wasn't certain that this was something that Granger would want to know, but it probably was. Still, it wouldn't hurt to run it by someone who worked with things like this. And Lyle knew Granger well enough to call her Al, short for Alice.

The woman out front seemed perplexed by Mark's response. I wanted to ask her when she'd started trying to reach her friend but that might put us in a position to break the guest's privacy.

Lyle responded to my text by calling.

"You have a guest who checked out the same day they checked in and now someone is asking about them?" he said. "There's more to this than you wrote isn't there?"

"Detective Penn was here earlier asking about a guest with the same, not super common, last name in conjunction with the man who was murdered in town last night," I said.

"You know about that?" he asked.

As if I never knew anything. While the hotel wasn't exactly in town, we did hear things. Mark lived in house a bit outside the main part of Glade Springs, but Suzanne had an apartment in town. And they weren't the only people I talked to.

"I attend classes at the dojo, remember," I said. I could have told Lyle I was the one to find the body but didn't want to worry him. Not that there was anything to worry about.

"Don't tell me you found the body," he said.

"Then I won't," I replied.

That was met with a big sigh.

"I'd tell the police if you can. Technically that might violate your privacy policy and it might have nothing to do with anything," he said.

We could tell someone that a person wasn't a guest and Nancy wasn't. Technically I could argue that. It seemed like the better part of valor to let the police know.

"Penn or Granger?" I asked.

"I'd talk to Al," Lyle said, "but you seem to get along better with Ed."

Which meant that Al had probably said something to Lyle and it hadn't exactly been favorable. Great.

Hanging up, I typed out a text to Detective Penn. I left out exact names but I knew he'd call.

Chapter Seven

Detective Penn didn't respond until after I'd gotten up and eaten some lunch downstairs. I got a call from Mark that Penn was waiting for me at the desk. I'd been enjoying the break with the two cats. Chai was sitting beside me and Latte was on my lap. The day was overcast and I'd turned on the gas fireplace in my apartment.

The empty bowl I had used for my soup was sitting on the coffee table in front of me. I'd finished that and was relaxing with the boys, trying to forget about the body I'd found. I was more upset that afternoon than I had been earlier, probably because I'd passed the point of exhaustion and, now, I was ruminating.

I was thankful for the brief retreat into my personal space. It wasn't large, just a front room with a small fireplace, a tiny galley kitchen that barely had room for two people, a bedroom and a bathroom. The saving grace was the storage space. I'd recently learned it had been built for Olive and she'd moved from a fairly large house. She probably needed the storage space even more than I did.

When my phone beeped to tell me I had a new text, the boys glared at me, perhaps anticipating that I would be getting up to leave.

"Sorry about that," I told them. The cats were not forgiving, not bothering to even look at me as I left.

Detective Penn was leaning against the edge of the receptionist desk when I got upstairs. I smoothed down my shirt over the black slacks I was wearing. It was more to give me a moment to figure out what to say than to smooth a wrinkle.

"Detective," I said as I walked up to him.

He didn't start, though he stood up a little straighter. Something about the way he moved gave me the impression that although he'd appeared not to see me at all, and was enjoying the music from the bar, perhaps doing a little people watching in that direction, he'd known I was there all along. He'd probably even noticed the momentary smoothing of the shirt. I hoped I hadn't gotten any grease or something on the plain maroon coloring.

"Ms. Davenport. I've been attempting to locate the conference organizer, this Logan Fulton. We've been unable to contact him either via a message from your desk, calls to his cell phone, or even looking around in your conference center. Can you at least verify that he's checked in?"

Mark nodded at me.

"I take it you've done that?" I asked Mark.

"I did. I can't give out a room number nor do we have any pictures. I've offered to contact Sissy McMason, but she may or may not be able to help," Mark said.

I shook my head. "Sissy doesn't keep track of people. She's just the person everyone calls if there's a problem with the event." Unless of course they found me first, which was always a possibility. The staff tended to forget about her, which was easy to do as her office was down by the spa area. While it was part of the hotel, not all the staff went down that direction regularly, unless they were housekeeping or security. We had conference rooms down there but those tended to be reserved for weddings and the largest of the conferences.

"Perhaps I could speak with you in private?" Penn asked nicely.

My heart started to pound. He was going to question me again. Of course, at least he wasn't doing that in front of any guests who might walk through the lobby. I took him back to my office.

Penn didn't look any more memorable in the cigarette smoke scented office I inhabited than he did anywhere else. I don't smoke but over the years other managers had. While it had been repainted, re-carpeted, and basically remodeled except for the oversized desk, the aroma hung around. I hated it and expected that it was linked to the desk, which was not exactly my favorite piece of office furniture.

However, the desk was too large to get through the door and given that it was all hard wood and probably hand-built in an era when such things were done, I had no desire to have it chopped for firewood. Nor, did I have the budget to smash through a wall no matter how much I might want to. A nice windowed wall would be wonderful, one with blinds so that I'd get more light in the office and still be able to get some privacy.

He sat in one of the chairs near the table and pulled out a tiny notebook.

"Remind me again why you were at the dojo last night?"
I told him.
He nodded.
"It seems like it would have been smarter to call the

owner? He says that the office number forwards to his cell phone. While he doesn't always answer, he does listen to messages in case it's something he needs to deal with."

"Brett said that it would take people all night to pull things out of the building. I figured even if I got there after the lockers had been removed, someone would be there. I didn't expect to be alone. There was a truck down in the parking lot behind the building when I arrived and I thought that maybe the workers had just taken a break to grab a late dinner."

"It was about eight o'clock when you arrived?" Penn repeated.

I nodded, though it had been a little before. I had left the hotel around seven, later than I liked. I am such a home-body. Of course, most of the shops in town, except for the grocery store, a few bars, and restaurants closed at six or seven. The dojo was always open until nine.

I added that in case it made a difference.

"But you knew that Brett wasn't having classes. He'd gotten lucky to be fit into the demolition schedule because they'd had a last-minute cancellation due to delays on another project," Penn said.

I hadn't known about the cancellation. Brett *had* gotten lucky. Chances were, if he hadn't, the dojo would have been closed for far longer.

"The worker that was killed wasn't part of the regular crew removing the interior furnishings that Brett wanted saved," Penn said.

"I didn't recognize him, though I hadn't seen any of them," I replied easily. I wasn't sure what he was getting at.

"Dale Benton," Penn said. "He's got a rather varied employment record. Picks up work here and there, often several part time jobs. This past summer he worked with the landscaping crew that worked at the Neary-Ten."

Of course. That gave me a connection to the man. Great.

"I have a facilities manager who takes care of things like the landscaping and the temporary hires we do for that," I said. "I oversee payments to the company, but if we contracted with them, I don't have names. My job often keeps me inside during the main part of the day so I rarely see the workers."

"I'm sure," Penn said. "It's just interesting that you found him. He worked here. And there are people who clearly knew him that are currently staying here."

Penn seemed to enjoy the slight discomfort I felt. It was less that I had something to hide and more that I feared he was building a case against me for murdering a man I didn't even know.

"I must have bad luck," I said. "Have you spoken with Mr. Ingles?"

Penn shook his head. "Like this Logan person, he's not been around. At least not that we can find. I have a feeling that the people at this conference are rather suspicious of law enforcement."

"Perhaps," I said. They did dress rather as if they were quite counter culture, although most were old enough to have to outgrown such things. I wondered what Sissy thought of them.

"I also got your message about the woman with the same name. We're attempting to find out who she might be. You said another guest was asking about her?"

"I'm not sure it was a guest. It might have been someone from town," I said. "I just know that this Nancy checked in yesterday afternoon and then checked back out around midnight."

Penn pursed his lips but said nothing.

I tried not to fidget.

Sighing, Penn finally put away his little notebook.

"It's not that we think you murdered him. It appears there was quite an altercation, probably a fight. Cause of death was a blow to the head. Unless you're far better at martial arts than Brett has suggested, it's unlikely that you could have done it. However, that doesn't mean you didn't see something."

I shrugged. "The only thing I can remember, other than the body, was the truck that was in the back. It was gone when I came out. And I heard someone come through the door. They didn't check in while I was talking to the 911 operator and no one came out when the police got there, so I think they were probably leaving the building while I was in the locker room."

Penn nodded. "I have that. Did you hear the way they walked? Notice anything other than it was a truck?"

I shook my head. "It wasn't a construction truck with stuff in the back. It was an ordinary truck, with no top. It didn't seem full."

"Color?"

"It was dark out so I couldn't tell. I think it was two toned, like brown on the bottom half and white on the upper half of the truck bed. Or maybe it was green or blue or even black?" I said, trying to remember.

Penn pulled his notebook back out and made that note. It was something I hadn't thought to add when Granger had asked. Of course, she hadn't pressed me about the truck. Last night, they'd probably been more focused on who the man was and what he was doing there.

Then he nodded and got up.

"We'll be in touch," he said. "In case you remember something else or if Fulton or Ingles—either of them—turns up."

Penn turned and left the room, leaving me sitting there wondering if he thought I was a good witness or if, his assurances to the contrary, he and Granger were looking at me for murder.

Chapter Eight

It took some time to calm myself after the police interview so that I could get a little work done. The aroma of cigarette smoke bothered me so much that it was all I could do to keep from running out of the office screaming, which, if Penn had stuck around, would have made me look incredibly guilty. Not that I was, of course.

Still, the room felt claustrophobic and far too warm, though it was normally comfortable. Olive showing up just then would have been a godsend. The chill she brought with her would have been exactly what I needed. Of course, there's never a ghost around when you need her.

I had been told she was working on her next book. Suzanne worked evenings transcribing the words. Fortunately, as Olive had no need for money—it's not like the dead can go on a shopping spree—Suzanne was getting all the royalties. Honestly, that was the main reason I was willing to be out there pretending to be Olive and signing books.

I looked up to see the gray-haired woman who claimed to be Olive's relative come out of the bar.

Suzanne was standing at the desk, checking on something. Vaguely, I heard Mark in the little printer area next to my office. If my office was a closet, that was barely a cupboard. Suzanne turned to ask me a question and I stood up, walking over to her, hoping not to be noticed.

Olive's relative was moving easily, carefree and clearly enjoying herself. She turned to look behind her and held up her hand in a wave. Then she looked at the desk. Our eyes met. The light joyous look in hers hardened into something else. The slight prance she'd had turned into a march as she came over to the desk.

"What are you doing here?" she snapped, almost as if she hadn't already said she knew I worked at the Neary-Ten. Maybe she thought I was pretending to do that, too.

"I'm the manager," I said. "Maggie Davenport. Nice to meet you." She'd seemed aware of that when I'd met her in the bookstore, so her question was odd.

"You think you can take over my cousin's life, don't you? Are you some sort of stalker?" she was angry again, color flooding her cheeks.

"I'm just here doing my job," I replied, trying to keep my voice even.

"You write books under my cousin's name. You take her job. You probably murdered her in her bed! It's what stalkers do!" the woman had raised her voice.

"Excuse me," Suzanne said. "I work on those books. It was my idea to write under Olive's name."

The gray-haired woman glared at her.

"Olive's life had so much input into the stories. We imagined what she'd do if she were still running the hotel." Suzanne talked far more calmly than I would have. Of course, she wasn't being accused of being a stalker, either.

However, it did give me some time to calm myself while Suzanne soothed and tried to smooth things over.

"I adored my cousin. And she was just gone!" the woman wailed.

I wanted to ask why she wasn't at the funeral, although I worried that would sound stalker-ish, although if anyone was stalking someone, it seemed she was doing so to me.

"And now here is this pathetic woman using her name to write books!" there were tears now. However, something about them didn't ring quite true.

"We had no idea that using Olive's name would be so upsetting," Suzanne placated.

"If you had close family, you'd understand. Olive was everything to us."

The woman was still sniffling, although learning that I wasn't alone as the author seemed to have taken something out of her. Or perhaps she was just trying to decide which of us she should be most angry with.

"I knew you worked here," she snapped at me. "But stealing Olive's position! It's like you're taking her life. Olive should still be here! Everyone loved her."

I bit back any number of comments, from the one about it being impossible to steal from the dead to the one about this woman not being at the funeral.

"And you," she pointed at Suzanne. "I can't believe you even met her! I can forgive that. You wouldn't know what a kind and generous woman she was. I'm waiting on a call from my attorney, though, to see what I can do about you using her name so blatantly. Don't expect that you'll see your next royalty check."

The woman turned away and marched off.

"Do you know who that was?" I whispered to Suzanne.

"No. I didn't check her in if she's staying here."

"She saw me signing books at the Cornered Reader. She had a fit then, too."

"I doubt that using a name would get us into trouble. It's a name. I think so long as Olive wasn't a famous writer, we should be okay."

"Worst case, maybe Olive could testify that it was her idea?" I giggled, wondering how that would go over.

I felt a chill as Olive wandered out from the office.

"And just what is it that you think I could testify about?" she asked. She was in her haughty mode, looking down her nose at us, though really, she wasn't all that much taller.

I took a moment to note the similarity to the woman claiming to be her cousin. There was definitely a family resemblance. As much as I hated to do it, I was going to have to ask Olive about her family life and hope that she remembered the most important things.

Chapter Nine

Suzanne and I gave each other a look. Mark came out of the little cubby where we stored things, and sometimes did paperwork, looking a bit uncomfortable. The bar music went to a slow 80s era ballad of some sort, giving the moment a bit of slowed dramatic tension.

"That woman said she was your cousin," I told Olive. "She's upset that I'm using your name to write my books. She's threatening to get an attorney to try and get the royalties."

"Cousin?" Olive looked perplexed.

"She didn't give a name."

Mark frowned. "I think she said it was something like Lyn or Lisa..." he trailed off. It's hard to recall names when you work with so many people coming and going. And it's not typically necessary.

"Liliane?" Olive asked.

Mark snapped his fingers and said, "Lily! That was it."

"She must have shortened the name then. It's really Liliane. She hated her name. Although why she thinks that you using my name is a problem, I don't know. Her mother and I spoke maybe once a year."

"They didn't help plan your funeral," I said. I winced as I said it, hoping that wouldn't be horrible for Olive to hear. I mean who hears about who came and who didn't come to their own funeral?

"I would be surprised if they did or if anyone showed up. I was never close to my family. We weren't locals. Most of my family is up in Pennsylvania. That's where Liliane lived as far as I know. Even though it wasn't terribly far, no one ever came to visit. And then I got divorced and they all practically disowned me. Liliane was a bit younger than me, closer to your age," Olive nodded at me. "You'd think she was Catholic or something talking about mortal sins and divorce."

"Divorce isn't a mortal sin," Mark said.

We all turned to look at him.

"Raised Catholic, though not practicing much now." He winced, probably wondering if that was too personal. "Sorry."

"Not at all," Olive said. "But that kind of thing was the dramatic sort of language Liliane liked to use. I'm not sure what church she was going to at the time. She changed churches like some of us changed our clothing. I have to say I didn't much like her even as a child."

"She's been telling me how you were her dear cousin Olive and she misses you greatly."

"Oh piffle!" Olive snapped. She said it loudly enough that a young person in a black cape turned to look over at us, startled. Seeing us talking, he shook his head and continued on towards the bar. Clearly here for the vampire lovers conference or whatever it was called.

"I take it that's not your impression," I commented.

"We were never close. The divorce was just an excuse for her to avoid ever having to call me again. It's not like today where you can be friends with your annoying family on Facebook and just not follow them."

I raised an eyebrow, surprised that Olive knew that much about Facebook.

Olive stared me down, daring me to question her. Perhaps Suzanne had suggested something as a plot point for one of the books. I certainly wasn't talking to her about social media, although perhaps I should have been.

"Well, I'm not sure how we counter that," I said.

"Check my will. I left everything to charity," Olive said. "The one for hearts."

She looked a bit confused for a second. I knew that sometimes she couldn't remember things from her life. Olive had told me that the longer she was a ghost the harder it was to remember certain things. Clearly, her cousin was something she remembered very well and not in a good way.

"They might claim that was an oversight?" Suzanne suggested. "It's not as if you can copyright a name or anything. The only real leverage she has against us is that we work in the hotel where you worked and we used your name. I'm not sure it's illegal."

Mark shrugged and turned back to the computer. He seemed unconcerned about our potential legal troubles, or at least the troubles of having Lily around.

Suzanne and Olive and I huddled discussing ways we could say this was an honor rather than a problem in case Lily really did bring a lawsuit.

At the front desk, two young women in dark clothing came up to the desk. I didn't hear exactly what they asked, but I did hear the name Logan.

I turned and frowned, wondering what was going on. Penn hadn't been able to find Logan Fulton. Nor Rory Ingles.

"What is it?" I asked Mark.

"They're asking me to ring the room for the conference organizer," Mark said. "I guess one of the speakers didn't show up."

I raised an eyebrow and waited while Mark dialed the room. I hoped that Logan answered. It seemed an odd thing that the organizer wasn't around. Sissy would have a cell number if no one responded in the room, although it was odd that there wasn't a secondary person to help out. Conferences took a lot of work and the organizer was always in demand.

No answer, but Mark left a message.

"You don't have his cell phone?" one of the women asked. She had dyed black hair, the sort that looks like someone rubbed shoe polish on it. Her friend was bleached blonde. Both had long straight hair that fell halfway down their backs.

"We don't," Mark said.

"I'll see if our events coordinator has it," I said, picking up the phone to call Sissy. I kept my back to the girls as I bit my lip, wondering what was going on and if this had anything to do with the dead man in the dojo.

Chapter Ten

The pop music got louder with a heavier beat that had me tapping my toes in something other than impatience as I listened to the ring on the other end of the phone. Mark was typing something on the computer. Suzanne was back looking at her terminal and Olive had wandered into the office leaving behind only the faintest chill.

I wiggled the fingers of one hand to get more blood flowing. The chill from Olive wasn't a frostbite level chill but it was enough that my fingers were uncomfortably cold when she stood as close to me as she had been. It wasn't really her fault. The area behind the reception desk wasn't meant for three people to stand around in a half circle whispering.

I listened to the ring of the phone on the other end. I was about to give up and started planning the message I would leave when Sissy picked up.

"Sissy McMason, Neary-Ten Events," she said pleasantly.

"It's Maggie," I said. "We're having trouble getting a

hold of Logan Fulton and I was wondering if you had a cell number for him."

I heard her shuffling papers.

"I had a hard time getting a hold of him several times during the planning. He was always late and seemed very unorganized for a conference planner," Sissy said. "I'd often have to leave multiple messages. I'm surprised the thing is still going on, but he got the payments in on the last day, in the last few hours before I was going to have cancel the event for non-payment at each stage."

We took a deposit, but then had dates for various larger deposits to be put down so we could reserve the space, special room rates, and any catering. Conference organizers often stressed about getting enough hotel rooms booked to get the rate we offered, but most of the time the attendees were good about doing that. I seemed to recall that this one had a lot of last-minute reservations, shortly before the window was closing for the lower rate.

"I recall the issue with reservations," I said.

"Yep. I'll text you his number," Sissy said. "I have it here. It's on my phone, too, but not my contacts, thank heavens."

I walked into my office as I was listening. I wanted to hear more.

"I take it it was more than just difficult to get a hold of him?" I asked.

"You wouldn't believe," Sissy said. "He wanted all the food we served there to be red to make it look like blood or raw meat. He didn't like the extra pricing for that claiming that all we'd need to do was add food coloring, which is not how it works for all food. And then he'd whine about the costs and how he couldn't afford things, even if it shouldn't have been coming directly out of his pocket. He also liked to talk down to me, as if I didn't actually know my job when it seemed like he was the one who didn't know his job."

"Does he work for a company where he does event planning, or was this something he was doing on his own?"

"Supposedly he works for a group associated with the conference. Their name is Vampire Love, just like the conference. I haven't heard of it, but their money's good and I had no problems with the finances—well, once Logan paid," Sissy said. "They have a website, but it's pretty basic. There's a forum attached to it, but it's a members-only kind of thing and I wasn't about to sign up."

Interesting.

"I should go. I'll give him a call on his cell and let him know that people are looking for him."

"Tell them good luck. I have a feeling if something went wrong, he won't be willing to take responsibility for it. It wasn't something we did, was it?" Sissy suddenly sounded worried.

"It sounds like a speaker didn't show up."

"Ah. Logan probably missed their payment deadline or didn't bother to check an email saying they weren't coming," Sissy said. "That sounds like Logan and he won't want to hear about it, but that's not my problem. If he tries to schedule an event again, I won't be so eager to get them accommodated. Especially not at this time of year."

We hung up and I tried Logan's cell phone.

It rang through to voicemail. I wondered if Detective Penn or Granger had gotten through to him. If not, it seemed odd that he was so unavailable.

I went out to tell the women that I'd left a message but Logan wasn't answering his cell either.

"Jerk," the first one said. "I mean he and Rory were

fighting last night but I can't imagine him just leaving. Logan maybe, but not Rory."

My mouth went dry. I wondered if they were talking about Rory Ingles, the man Detective Penn was looking for in conjunction with the murder. I was going to have to start sleuthing to find a few answers just in case the hotel was dragged into this investigation after all. I did not need the negative publicity, not that the publicity about the other deaths had caused us any problems. It was one good thing about a haunted hotel. However, if murders became a regular issue, well even the bravest folks might start having second thoughts about booking.

Chapter Eleven

The girls left and I went back to my office. I should have been getting back to work, but now I wanted to know more about Rory. I also had a name for the dead man which I hadn't looked up. I had a lot of little things I could search. Maybe one of them would lead me to a clue.

I couldn't really see how someone here, at a conference, could have been involved with a murder in town. Penn had said Ingles was there to see Dale Benton. But our records showed the man was here for the Vampire Love conference, which every time the name crossed my mind struck me as ridiculous. Who wanted to love a dead person, or even an undead person? I just hadn't gotten into the vampire thing, I guess.

At any rate, there was the other person with the same last name as Rory who had left after only a few hours. That would have been odd even if she hadn't shared his last name. A sister? A wife? An ex-wife?

I started my search. The office was quiet but for the

music and occasionally a burst of laughter from in the lobby or in the bar area. I kept my head down, appearing to do my work, but actually doing some sleuthing. I'd done this before when I was distracted by events and it always left me with a pile of catch-up work when things had resolved themselves. It was annoying but I just couldn't seem to focus on my real work.

First, I searched Dale Benton. It wasn't a common name, but common enough that I needed more information to work with. He worked in Glade Springs, so I added that which limited the searches quite a bit.

There wasn't much information about Benton. He had a Facebook page but that was it. The page either wasn't active or it wasn't viewable by people who weren't his friends. He had a few of them but no one I knew. The names weren't even familiar. Being a small town, although I'd worked at the hotel for nearly thirty years now, I was something of a relative newcomer. Of course, it didn't help that I lived out at the hotel and for many years had only gone into town for a book or groceries. That was changing, but I still didn't know a lot of people. I relied on my workers for that.

A single article had Benton helping out at the local pancake breakfast. He'd been one of the many people who had set up tables for the high school fundraiser. This was a small article from within the last year. It was impossible to know if he always did that or if this was a new thing.

I searched his name through the local paper, which was online only now, but there were only two other mentions. One was Benton taking part in a dart tournament a few years ago and one because he'd donated a prize for a local church's fundraiser. He seemed like the kind of guy you called when something needed doing and that was it.

Of course, there could be more to the story but I didn't have it. Neither did the papers. I'd have to ask Mark or Suzanne if they knew Dale. They ran in completely different social circles in town so there was a good chance one of them knew something about him.

Next, I put in Rory Ingles name. I didn't know where he was from so when I got a long list of hits, it was difficult to know which might be him. I tried Nancy and Rory Ingles together, hoping that perhaps something would come up.

I found an obituary from a town in Virginia listing the two of them as survivors of a Mitchell Ingles. The two were siblings as far as I could tell from the wording. Based on Mitchell's age and the fact he appeared to be their father, both of them should only be a few years younger than I was, which seemed old for this conference. Of course, Mitchell might have had children late in life. Not having seen either of them, it was impossible to know.

Sighing, I knew I wasn't getting anywhere. I went back to my real work, making a few notes on some of the orders. I returned some calls and emails.

When my stomach started growling again and I began to think of heading down for dinner, I realized I'd never searched Logan Fulton's name. I could do that. I could even do it with a clear conscious as I had gotten my work done during the day.

Sissy had input Logan's contact information, including an address into the system. As her system wasn't about guests exactly, I felt less guilty about looking up the state where he lived. He was from a small town in Michigan.

I was a little surprised that the Neary-Ten was on his list of places to try and have a conference, but perhaps we were the closest interesting place that he hadn't tried to work with. Given what Sissy said, I wouldn't be surprised if other places refused to work with him or weren't willing to be accommodating. Sissy wouldn't be next time.

He had several social media profiles. All showed a man in who looked to be in his thirties. He had pale, fleshy skin on his face. Dark hair, though not dyed as dark as many of the people downstairs. He was wearing a black t-shirt and had his arms crossed across his chest rather like he was in a coffin or something. He was not smiling, though I could see the beginnings of a smirk.

I looked through photos and posts on the website. Fulton wasn't the president of Vampire Love. He was just the event coordinator. When he wasn't working on that, it appeared he did something in IT. That probably explained the pale skin. He was very into gaming and everything supernatural, which was probably how he had discovered the Neary-Ten.

There were a few photos of him mock biting other people. The same group seemed to be together and it was much smaller than the group downstairs. They were running around a city that could have been anywhere in the Midwest but no one had tagged the location. So much for my sleuthing skills.

He had locked down his friends list so I couldn't tell if he were friends with Rory online or not. I hadn't found images of Rory at all so I had no idea if he were part of the group. Again, I went back to the age thing. Probably not, but I couldn't be certain.

Sighing, I leaned back and rubbed my eyes. I wasn't getting anywhere. I needed to talk to people. Standing up, I went out to talk to Mark. Suzanne was ready downstairs helping Olive. Time had gotten away from me despite my lack of answers.

I realized I had also planned to talk to Dori, but she'd be busy with the dinner rush now, so no sense going down to the restaurant. Whenever I got distracted by a murder, things seemed to get completely out of control. Perhaps Mark would know something.

Chapter Twelve

ark and one of our part-timers were helping people at the desk. Mark was answering questions. The part-timer was checking in an older couple. From the way they were dressed, in dark blue jeans, pressed so that there was a crease down the front, with solid walking shoes that were not athletic wear, I suspected they were here for the fall leaves.

We weren't quite at peak leaf yet, but the woods were beautiful. I enjoyed looking out my window in the mornings, seeing how the world had changed each day with the leaves getting more gold and orange and even some brown. The branches started to peek out, showing off the various browns of their bark while the evergreens became more prominent now that the world wasn't a palette of greens.

The bar was doing a brisk pizza business tonight and the smell was wonderful as it wafted towards me. It might have been perfect if the evening had been slower and I could have talked to Mark about Dale Benton. Not that there was any guarantee that he would know Dale, but I could have crossed that off my list of things to find out.

I waved at the two of them and headed over to the bar. If I were lucky, Teri would be on shift at the bar and I could chat with her about Dale. The bar had no hostess and the seating was first come, first served even at dinner. Unfortunately, there were no seats, even at the bar. I didn't see anyone in black, which surprised me. They took up a significant part of the hotel capacity just then. On a weeknight, we didn't get a lot of people from town, unless someone had decided to hold an impromptu event.

Teri was serving like crazy but she nodded at me when she caught my eye. I nodded back and left the area. I didn't need pizza, although having smelled it, I wanted some. Sighing, I turned and headed downstairs. Teri would probably work until closing so I could return later. But for now, I needed to feed the cats.

The Vampire Love conference was still going strong. I heard plenty of laughter from the main conference room. The carts outside told me that it had been turned into a dining area. A couple of my workers were busily tidying up plates and cups. Neither paid me any attention. I walked quickly down the hallway and reached my apartment.

Both the cats were back on the sofa, or perhaps they'd never left. You never know with cats. Chai yawned at me and stretched. Latte immediately leaped up, ready for dinner. This was their main concern when I was late. While they always had a bit of kibble lest the hunger overcome them and they faint from what they considered starvation, I served wet food morning and evening and they lived for the good stuff.

I took care of that chore and was trying to decide what to make for my own dinner. Life would be simpler if I could just open a can of random people food and dump it in a bowl. Come to think of it, I probably could. It just wouldn't taste very good. Not like pizza with a thick crust and flavorful toppings.

My mouth watered and I considered calling in an order to go. I could eat some tonight and finish it over the next couple of days. I took out my phone only to have it ring, startling me.

The number was from the Cornered Reader. I frowned and answered.

"This is Maggie," I said.

"Clay from the bookstore," Clay said. He sounded nervous.

"What's up?" I asked.

"I just wanted to let you know that that woman was here again. I caught her pulling pages out of one of the books you signed. I've had to move them behind the counter now, which I hate doing because I want you to sell," Clay said. "Have you heard from any more from her?"

"I know her name is Lilianne, although she goes by Lily," I said. "I didn't get a last name." Olive's last name was Hughes but I had no idea if Lily had the same last name.

"I guess that's something," Clay said. "I'm not sure if I should keep her from coming back to the store or not."

"I'd suggest she not," I said. "You can let your employees know. She damaged your merchandise!" That annoyed me. Clay was a small bookstore owner and it wasn't like his profit margin was all that high.

"That's true," Clay said. He paused and then changed the subject. "I heard you found Dale."

"The man in the dojo?" I asked. It sounded as if Clay wanted to know more about that. I wondered if he knew something, or perhaps Bill did. I considered driving into town again tomorrow though I didn't actually need anything, but I could stop in and talk to both of them.

"Yeah, him," Clay said. His voice was flat as if he didn't even like talking about Dale.

"I did," I said. "Were you friends?"

Clay barked out a laugh. "No. Dale was a jerk. He liked to show up for fund raisers but when we were in high school, he stole the money from our school's fundraiser for the senior party. We ended up just having fruit punch in the gym and someone's older brother played music for us."

"That's horrible." I wondered if Dale had stolen something from someone else on the demolition crew.

"It's why he always did one-off jobs. No one really trusted him with anything more. This way he did the work, got paid, and was sent off on his way. Harder to take advantage, though I know he did. There are a couple of construction contractors who won't hire him on any of their crews," Dale said.

More and more interesting. Dale appeared to have more enemies than I thought.

"Wow. I wonder if someone from the crew did it," I said.

"Doubtful. I know the other guys doing the demo, too. They might not have liked Dale, but they aren't the sort to kill someone. And if they did, they'd have been smart enough to hide the body better."

I didn't add that perhaps they weren't expecting anyone when I came in. I remembered the truck that had been behind the building when I arrived. Maybe I interrupted someone planning to hide the body. That thought made me shudder.

"But did you know everyone on that crew?" I asked.

Clay was silent for a moment. "Probably."

It was too bad that I didn't know the color of the truck I saw. I had described it to the police but it had been too dark to see clearly. It wasn't a bright color like red. Maybe if I went into town to look at trucks one of them would look familiar. But that would be for tomorrow when I had better light.

"But I just wanted to warn you that this woman is really going after you. Be careful," Clay warned. "I don't like that she's willing to tear up books. She seems really angry. It's hard to imagine that after all this time she still carries such grief for her cousin. Maybe they grew up together?"

"Olive would have been much older," I said. "She was older than my mother when we worked together." Not by a lot, really, but by almost two years. The cousin wasn't much older than I was, if that. I should have asked if Olive recalled Lily's age.

"Maybe she saw her as a mother figure."

"Maybe," I said, though I doubted it. Olive would have remembered that. And I had a feeling if Olive had children, or even someone she thought of as a child, she would have showed photos and talked about them until everyone was sick to death of hearing about them. She was rather like that with her book babies.

Clay and I rang off and I was left with plenty to think about, not the least of which was the information he'd given me about Dale. Tomorrow, I was definitely driving into town to look at trucks and see if I recognized one.

Chapter Thirteen

Going into town remained my plan until I got a phone call in the early morning hours. It was a few minutes before my alarm was due to go off and I was snuggled down under my thick burgundy covers enjoying the last bits of warmth before I had to get up and get moving. The boys were snuggled with me, one on either side, their body heat keeping me warmer than just the blanket. I was still softly drowsy, not having remembered all the things I needed to get done or the troubling information about the murder.

Looking at who was calling, I was unsurprised to see Addy's name. However, anything that made her call me this early didn't mean anything good.

"What's up?" I asked even before saying my name. Addy knew she was calling me.

"We have an issue," Addy said. "There's a group of people insisting that no one has seen Logan Fulton since yesterday and they want what one of them calls a welfare check on his room. I'm not authorized to do that if there's no real reason to check. Housekeeping was there yesterday morning so it's a bit early."

"The police have been attempting to get him as well," I said. "In this case, have the people asking wait a few minutes and I'll be up."

"Thanks," Addy said.

Addy was perfectly capable of going upstairs and checking the room if necessary. I could have told her to do it while I got dressed and planned for the day, but given that the police were searching for Logan, I felt I ought to do the room check. Perhaps I should have let Addy do it to avoid appearing like a ghoul if he were also found dead, something I passionately hoped was not the case, but I felt a need to protect her from having to see such a thing.

I went through a minimal level of cleaning my teeth to get rid of my morning breath and combing the main snags out of my hair. I dressed quickly and fed the cats, mindful that if I did find something in Logan's room, I'd be gone for some time. Chai and Latte were more than pleased to eat their stinky food early. I hoped they didn't think this would become a habit. I did not want to have to start getting up half an hour earlier to feed them at their preferred time.

The conference area was quiet. I had a brief wait at the main elevator which I took to the next floor. It was a testament to how tired I was that the stairs seemed overwhelming. It was only then that I wondered why two people from a conference like Vampire Love, which went well into the late hours, were asking at the desk about the organizer at this time of the morning.

A handful of people milled around the lobby. Some were heading into the café for breakfast. A couple were sitting near the doors with luggage, probably awaiting a ride.

A woman got off the elevator next to mine and walked towards the doors. Typical early morning at a hotel as people finished up their vacation or their business in town, not that we had many business travelers.

At the desk I looked at the two women. They were the same women who had asked the night before.

"Still haven't found him?" I asked.

They shook their heads. "I know Logan is a flake, but he and Rory were really angry with each other," the one said. She looked tired.

"I'm surprised you're up this early."

"It was just a big party last night. We were supposed to have speakers but nothing was going as planned. No one knew where they were supposed to be. And Logan was definitely not around. He's helped out with other conferences and it's not been this bad, so it's kind of worrying."

I noticed the way she said helped out. I wondered if there was another person who was supposed to work with Logan to keep the conference running. I didn't ask more, though. I couldn't be certain that what the girl was telling me wasn't just gossip. Besides, worry ate at my insides. I'd gone upstairs to check a room before and found a body. I had no desire to do so again.

Pressing the up button for the elevator, a pair of the silvery doors opened almost immediately. I stepped inside, the girls following me. They probably should have waited downstairs, but I couldn't order them not to come upstairs. Logan was on the fifth floor. The soundless ride wasn't just smooth but fast. I hated slow elevators and kept ours in excellent working order.

The girls went silent in the little box. It was just the three of us and they'd been doing plenty of talking before. It was interesting how the slight change in scenery changed the dynamic of what was going on. Or perhaps, having convinced someone to check on Logan, the young women didn't feel a need to say more.

The fifth floor was quiet. Our feet made no noise on the speckled blue carpet. The carpet was clean though the padding was getting a bit worn under my feet. I'd have to look into how expensive it would be to redo the carpets throughout. It wouldn't be cheap but in the next few years it would probably be best to get it done. Perhaps I could start some sort of improvement fund. I'd send a note to Ari about it. If we put aside some funding specifically for the flooring, it probably wouldn't hurt quite as much when it came time to have it done.

We passed a room that had a television on low. I could make out the low drone of voices with a hint of music. I supposed it could have been someone playing their music and talking but chances were, it was a TV.

Logan's room was halfway down the long side of the hall on the fifth floor. Our elevators were annoyingly not central to the hotel. That had happened thanks to the expansion and the Bowmans ending up trying to cut costs by not moving the elevators or installing another bank. Olive had done her best to try and talk them into doing so, but they'd held firm thinking that changing the placement would ruin the look of the lobby.

I knocked on the plain cream-colored door and waited. No answer. I knocked a bit louder.

"Logan?" I called. I didn't yell. It was far too early and I knew there were other conference goers around.

I heard nothing from behind the door.

Someone opened the door behind me.

"Would you guys let it go. He's not there! And some of us actually want to sleep!" The young man, brown hair tousled from sleep, stood in the doorway. His gray sweats had a stain on one thigh and he was shirtless, the pasty white of his hairless, soft chest on full view.

Seeing me, he backed off.

"They've been noisy," he said before closing his door rather softly.

No one had come to the door.

"Hotel management coming in," I called. I tried to keep my voice soft but I had to speak in at least a normal volume so that someone would hear me.

I waited a few moments, listening. Nothing inside.

Someone flushed a toilet on the sixth floor, the water in the plumbing rushing through the pipes above my head.

When no one answered, I used my passkey. My stomach was in knots. I did not want to find another body. The room was dark. It stank but it was the stink of rotten food, not the metallic scent of blood or the putrid smell of bodily waste.

I stepped in, motioning the young women to stay back. I found the light and turned it on. No one groaned or complained. The room was an ordinary room, with a bathroom to my right, the door partly closed, a small closet on my left and then the main part of the room. A single king-size bed sat a few feet from the bathroom wall, a side table next to it. A television hung on the wall across and beside the TV area was a small desk with a handful of drawers and a mini refrigerator that was more of a cooler than anything. A single green chair with a footstool was angled in the corner.

The bed was messy but no body waited on it. I looked

on the far side by the chair. No body lay on the floor, either. I came back out and checked the bathroom. No one waited in a blood-soaked tub and the shower was off, though every towel left in the room was on the floor.

Logan was definitely a slob. I checked the little closet where we kept the ironing board, which was now rarely used, and the stand for a suitcase. No one stuffed in there, either.

The room was empty of a human being.

The young women had crowded into the entry and were trying to see everything I was doing.

"No one is here," I said. Which was something of a relief, although it left me with the mystery of where Logan was. And Rory Ingles. I wondered if the detectives had gotten a hold of him.

I stepped out and made sure everyone was out of the room before pulling the door closed.

"Now what?" one of the young women said. She looked at me as if I were the person who should know.

"I suppose you could report him as a missing person to the police," I said. "But he's not in his room which is all I can do."

"You mean you can't go room by room to make sure someone didn't kill him in their room?" one of the women said.

"I cannot go searching every room," I said.

"But you have a master key! That would be so much easier. The police won't take us seriously."

"But they're your only option. I run a hotel, not a private investigative service."

If I could find the photo I'd seen earlier of Logan, perhaps I could get Olive to go searching through the hotel to see if she could find him. I wasn't going to mention that to the two young women. I didn't need them calling out for Olive, hoping to make her appear. If there was a way to make sure Olive didn't do something, it would be by telling her she had to do it.

Chapter Fourteen

I finally persuaded the two women to call the police themselves. I really wasn't the person who ought to do it. No doubt our local detectives were aware that Logan couldn't be found, but perhaps a phone call from worried friends would make the police do a more intensive search for him. It was certainly possible that Logan was sleeping off a hangover in someone else's room, which wasn't a crime. It did, however, sound as if there was a reason to be concerned.

It was difficult to remember that so long as he hadn't been harmed on site or found to be committing a crime at the hotel, it wasn't really my business. It was up to the police to find him. I tried to remind myself of that as I plodded down the hallway to my apartment. I still needed a shower and to have some coffee, and probably a bit of breakfast.

The cats were both settled on the sofa when I entered. Recently fed, they only turned to stare at me with their blue eyes and flick their brown ears when I entered. This was clearly not part of their routine. As they weren't dying of hunger, my intrusion on their morning bird watching and napping was a minor annoyance.

My apartment smelled only faintly of coffee and that seemed wrong. I yawned, trying to decide if I wanted coffee or a shower first. It would be nice to have a cup waiting for me but I worried that if I made coffee and sat down, I'd forget to shower completely, so I went in to do that first.

Ablutions done, coffee and toast made, I sat down on the sofa and tried to think. My phone rang. The number wasn't familiar but as manager, I usually answer in case it's someone from around the hotel. Mostly that serves me, particularly, when like this number, the area code is local.

This time, however, the call was from Detective Granger.

"We've had a report that this conference organizer is missing," Granger said. "What do you know about it?"

As if I had all the answers. I told her honestly that I'd been contacted early that morning by the two young women. We went up to his room and he wasn't there.

"He's not checked out," Granger confirmed.

He hadn't. I had a feeling if he had and if the conference goers knew, they'd have been more than a little angry.

"Is his car there?"

"It's not something we've checked on," I said. We did get a license plate from our guests but I hadn't gone out and looked for a car. "He's not local so I guess I thought perhaps he had taken a shuttle."

It would have been better if she'd called the front desk.

"I need you to check."

"I can go do that. I'll call you back when it's done."

"Don't you have computers that can do it quickly?" Granger demanded.

"I'm not at a computer," I said. I mean, I suppose technically I was. My phone had a computer and I had my laptop but I wasn't at a computer hooked into the hotel's system.

A deep sigh.

"I would have thought that it was too early for you to be running around the building."

"It is," I said. "Although I was awakened early this morning by the two young woman who reported Logan Fulton missing and now I'm back in my apartment getting ready for the day. I realize this makes me a bit late, but we do have other managers who can assist you in getting your information."

"Your attitude isn't helping your case," Granger snapped and hung up.

I was so annoyed that Chai meowed at me, perhaps wondering what was wrong. I reached out to pet him, hoping that would calm me. Granger had acted as if I were the problem and not her. Like I had something to worry about. It irritated me that she seemed to think I was involved in everything that went wrong in town.

Just when I'd thought that a missing person wouldn't have anything to do with me, she had to go and make me feel as if I were the reason Logan had disappeared.

Sighing, I finished my coffee. Latte stretched out a little when I got up. Both cats watched me wash the mug and then head towards the door. Neither seemed too upset. Chai had already laid his head back down for a snooze.

While it was getting towards midmorning, the doors to the main conference room were open. A few people milled around. All of them seemed to be carrying the largest sized coffees we sell. The event had gone late last night even without the organizer. I glanced at the schedule and noticed they were still about an hour early for the first morning events. If Logan wasn't around, I wondered if the sessions were still happening.

This really wasn't my problem. I pushed the concerns about unhappy conference attendees out of my mind. We could offer them some drink vouchers if people complained to us. We were not the ones planning the event. We were merely coordinating with their planner. If that planner wasn't available, we could only pick up so much slack.

By the time I reached the lobby, I made up my mind to give Sissy a call and let her know that she might be doing more work for this event than expected. Perhaps she could help the assistant planners with anything that needed doing. Heck, she might even have a phone number for someone who might know what was going on with Logan.

I glanced the clock but didn't think she'd be in her office yet, so I went down to the café to grab another cup of coffee. I had a feeling I was going to be drinking several of those.

Chapter Fifteen

When I headed back to the desk, Mark signaled that there was someone on hold for me. I sighed. Suzanne was working on something nearby and gave me a sympathetic look. The coffee had perked me up and, from her look, I knew that it was probably Detective Granger. I had said that we would look and see if the car was in the lot. I hadn't done that yet.

"Is it Granger?" I asked. I kept my voice soft, pitching it just loud enough to be heard over the soft music that wafted through the speakers.

The lobby was warmer than some other parts of the hotel because the fire was going in the fireplace already. I loved the fall days when we had a fire. It made the place feel cozier than I'd expect from the sterile white of floors and walls.

"It is," Mark said.

"Give her the license number and ask one of the bell-hops to go out and see if they see it in the lot." I continued on my way, hoping that was all it was. Mark hung up the phone and nodded at me when I came back behind the desk having had to walk all the way around it to get to the little entry area.

"Thanks. She called me on my cell," I said.

"She's difficult," Suzanne said, commiserating. She was typing something into the computer.

I looked over her shoulder. It was a note about a charge on Rory Ingles' room.

"Rory Ingles," I said. "Did he do something?"

"Housekeeping was there this morning. Several towels are missing. He hasn't checked out, but they wanted me to make a note that this is the second time they've gone in and cleaned only to find all the towels are missing. He even asked for extras. They have the numbers down there."

The missing towels were odd.

"Did anyone talk to him?" I asked.

Suzanne shook her head. "I just talked to house-keeping."

"Make a note for them that if he gets back to them, he needs to contact the police. They're looking for him." My head was starting to throb a bit. I had too many people who appeared to not want to be found wandering around the hotel. Then there was the dead man I had found in town, which reminded me, I had planned to drive into town and look around at trucks to see if any looked familiar.

First, though, I really needed to drink my coffee. I wasn't nearly awake enough to go driving. I settled into my office, breathing deeply to try and calm my nerves. I'd rarely felt so irritable about things and much worse had happened in the hotel and to me.

I rubbed my temples just as I heard a man asking for me at the desk. Standing up and peering around the door I saw that it was Lyle. He held a cup of coffee in his hand. I'd probably just missed him walking into the café, unless he'd been seated and was finishing up.

Walking out, I went to the desk.

"How can I help you?" I asked.

"So formal," Lyle teased. "I wanted to be sure you were still okay after finding the man in the dojo."

"I am. We've had a bit of a mess with this conference, though, and I think I'm getting a headache." I needed to take something for it. I could feel it pounding in my temple and starting to crawl up and down my neck.

"Vampire Love. Who could have guessed that would be a problem?" Lyle asked.

Suzanne snorted. Mark smiled but kept quiet.

"I heard that they brought Brett Evans, the building owner, in for questioning about the dead man," Lyle said. "I know he was your teacher and all, but my sources say that the detectives like him for it. I guess Dale was stealing stuff from the lockers there as he did the work. The story is that the vic returned to the dojo in hopes of finding something else left behind that he could take before anyone noticed."

"I can't believe Brett would kill someone," I said.

Lyle gave me a look. I sighed. I didn't actually know Brett. He was just someone I liked.

"I would hate for it to turn out to be him," I said quietly.

Lyle and I chatted for a few minutes before he headed out to work. I went back to my office. Olive was lingering around the bookshelves. She turned when I entered.

"Well?" she asked.

"Well what?"

"Is anyone else dead? What have I missed. I got so involved in my book that I think I worked all night after

Suzanne went home. I just dictated and dictated. Of course, the conference goers were distracting out in the hallway. They went far later than they normally do. And they did not seem particularly happy. The hotel will get blamed, of course, even if, from what I could gather, it's not really our fault."

I rubbed the side of my head again as I told her what I knew about Logan.

"Another mystery."

"Lyle seems to think that the detectives think Brett murdered the man in the dojo." I sighed as I said that. I found some ibuprofen in the desk drawer. I glanced at the outdate and noticed it was a few months past. I hoped that it still worked enough to at least take the edge off of this headache. Too much thinking and not enough sleep.

Olive nodded her head. She was clearly thinking.

"You know Brett. Do you really think he'd be so careless as to leave the dead body in his building?"

"No. I just know him as a teacher. I don't know him, well, like could he have killed someone. But even so, maybe I interrupted something?" I suggested. I reminded her about the disappearing truck.

"Does Brett drive a truck?"

I shook my head. I'd seen him pull out of the dojo parking area a few times. He drove an older Mustang, not a fancy one, but one that looked like he picked it up at a less than reputable used car lot and was hoping it would continue to run. I thought it looked to be about 20 or so years old, so it certainly wasn't a classic car, either.

"How do they think he got to the dojo then?" Olive demanded.

"The police must know something," I said. "While I

don't like her, I have heard that Granger is a good detective."

Olive sniffed and walked out to the desk. I watched as she stood around staring at people.

I had forgotten to tell her about the search for Logan Fulton, the conference organizer. I got up and went out to her. She was watching Suzanne, who was on the phone talking to someone.

"I forgot to mention, that it seems our conference organizer is missing. People are becoming concerned," I said. "I don't suppose you can check around the hotel to see if there's anyone who looks as if they're injured or hurt? If I can find the photos I saw, I'll show them to you."

I was too tired to remember where I'd seen them.

"I looked him up last night." I tried to mentally retrace my search steps for an instant.

Having thought of something, I hurried back to the computer, with Olive gliding after me. I searched Logan's profile again. I found the photos from one the events where he supposedly helped. I showed Olive the image of the dark-haired man, slightly portly, but not overly so.

"I suppose I can search for him," she said. "People are worried something has happened?"

"A couple of the event goers have even reported it to the police, though I'm not sure what good that will do. It's just odd that we have several missing people that could be connected to the death in town. Rory Ingles had an altercation with Logan, if you believe the young women, and we can't find him or Logan. And then there's a woman named Nancy Ingles who checked in the afternoon the conference started and then checked out at around midnight that same day, not even staying a full day," I said.

"It is unusual," Olive said. "I'll see if I can't spot this Logan person around the hotel."

She stared at me as if daring me to watch her pop out. I got up and went to talk to Suzanne. I really ought to tell her I'd be leaving to go into town. I wanted to look for a truck looking like the one I'd seen.

Chapter Sixteen

The phone rang again as I walked out, the shrill ring of it startling me. I probably needed more caffeine, or perhaps less caffeine and more sleep. The headache that was pounding the side of my head was getting stronger. I needed the pain medication to work quickly. The white tiles seemed to reflect what sun there was in the overcast sky into my eyes making it hard to keep them open.

Mark got the phone before I did which was a relief. However, he immediately put it on hold and said that there was someone on the phone for me.

I picked it up.

"This is Maggie Davenport," I said.

"Ms. Davenport, I represent Ms. Liliane Campbell. We need to sit down and arrange a meeting to see if we can come to an agreement of how to split royalties with her as you're using her cousin's name for your books. Given your history of working with Olive Hughes, it's clear you weren't just picking a name out of a hat, but were rather using her name to influence connections and readership, which is not legal."

"Exactly what is your name?" I asked. The soft music in the lobby turned to an old tune with a catchy beat which the pounding in my head seemed to pick up. I rubbed my temple hoping to ease it until I could get downstairs and take something.

"Morgan McDaniel," he said. "I work out of Raleigh. I'd like to suggest a meeting tomorrow afternoon."

"I can't possibly get to Raleigh tomorrow," I said. "That's hours away from here."

"Then I'm afraid I'll have to file a suit if you aren't even willing to sit down with someone."

"I'll be contacting an attorney," I said. "No matter if we sit down or if you file a suit."

"Then I suppose we'll see you in court, unless of course the judge just orders you to pay us."

He hung up the phone.

Now I had to find an attorney to represent me in a case that was clearly a money grab on the part of Lily or Liliane. I marched back to my office. I paused a moment, trying to decide what to do. My head continued to throb. The ibuprofen I'd taken was definitely taking its time working.

I called down to Jake, the head of our security. I probably should have been talking to him about the missing people anyway.

When he answered, I gave him the details of the missing people and asked him to have people keep an eye out. The conference goers had badges with names. If they saw a Logan or a Rory, perhaps that would be helpful.

"I'll get on it," Jake said, preparing to ring off.

"One last thing, the attorney Ari got you a few months ago, do you have their contact information? It seems that a relative of Olive's is attempting to sue me for using her "beloved cousin's" name."

"Eric is a criminal defense attorney. I doubt he'd take a case like that. I'll send Ari a message and see if she knows someone better suited to this kind of thing," Jake said. "Although it's too bad you can't get someone here to have Olive testify to the fact that she really is writing those books."

"She says that she and Lily hardly saw each other and basically when Olive divorced, Lily all but disowned her. I know Ari and I planned the funeral services when Olive passed. No family attended though we tried our best to notify them," I said.

"Sad," Jake said. "And probably a money grab. I'll get on it. If you don't get an email from me in the next few hours, call me. Or check in with Ari. She's the one with connections."

I agreed to do so. It also sounded like Jake and Ari were still an item. While there was a rather large age difference, Ari being slightly older than me and Jake perhaps fifteen years younger at least, they'd been dating. It had come out a few months ago when Ari's younger brother Floyd had been found dead in the hotel.

Sighing, I took in a few deep breaths. At least Jake was reliable and likely to get back to me fairly quickly. And Ari would be on my side. I had no doubt she'd get me a good attorney.

I sipped my coffee, letting the warmth flow down my throat, enjoying the flavor as it burst on my tongue and continued waking my tastebuds and brain cells. And maybe, just maybe the caffeine would help my headache, though I didn't hold out a lot of hope for that. I'd have to wait on the ibuprofen.

Work waited for me on my computer, but the idea of thinking was a bit much with the way my head felt. I put the computer to sleep so that someone would need to log in again, and then left my office.

"I'm going to be out for awhile this morning," I told Mark. "Can you handle it?"

He nodded.

Suzanne gave me a worried look.

"Is it about the pen name? I can't believe Olive has family that would do that!"

"Not really," I said. "I just need to get out. Jake is contacting Ari for me. Hopefully she'll have the name of an attorney."

The phone in my office rang, the direct line, then. I went back and answered.

"Maggie, how dare they?!" Ari was clearly upset about what was going on with the pen name thing.

"I suppose that someone thinks this is a good way to get money. Not that I have anything to do with the money. It's all in Suzanne's name. I just sign the books."

Ari began to laugh.

"And Olive actually wrote it, of course," Ari said. "I read it. And it was better than I expected. Olive never struck me as particularly creative."

"She's writing another one now," I said.

"Excellent. She could do quite well. I'm surprised the attorney didn't already look into who got the money for the books. You'd think they'd want that."

"The woman who came here claims that Olive was her beloved cousin. Olive says that Lily basically disowned her when Olive got her divorce."

Ari chuckled. "Olive was always on such poor terms with her whole family. I think that's why she stuck it out with her bastard of a husband for so long. You weren't around when she was married, but she was desperately unhappy. Even I could see that and I was hardly ever around her. I'm glad that she's found a friend now, even if she had to die to do it."

Which was probably the saddest commentary on any life that I'd heard. I sniffed a little, not completely from allergies or a runny nose, not that I would admit it to anyone.

"I'm texting you the name of the firm we use. They should have someone who can deal with the attorney who contacted you. I'll make sure the business pays and if they don't, I will. I've always been happy with your management and Jake speaks very highly of you as a boss."

I could tell that latter part was quite important to Ari. At least the two of them were still happy together.

"I'll look for it," I said. "And I didn't expect that you'd pay for it. I thought that maybe the royalties would help defray the cost. And Suzanne could claim it as a tax write off."

"Oh, so can we," Ari assured me. "And we probably need it more than she does! Of course, with her family, maybe she does need it. But nevertheless, let me do this. It makes me feel good to stick it to Olive's family because they weren't there for her when she needed them."

I agreed, although I had no idea who Suzanne's family was. I knew they had enough money to make major donations around the town, but it never occurred to me that Suzanne would have her own money. She seemed like such a hard worker. I half thought that if she were just there to keep busy, she wouldn't be willing to work full time, but what did I know?

The text came through almost immediately and I called

the firm. Ari had already told the secretary to expect my call and I was put through to one of the paralegals who took my information and the information I had about Morgan McDaniel.

She chuckled when I gave her the name. I knew that the law firm the Bowmans used was based in New York but they had a Raleigh office.

"McDaniel is an ambulance chaser, basically," the paralegal said. "We'll draft a response letter telling him to send any motions or questions directly to us. If he calls you again, send him to our firm." She gave me her name and the name of the attorney she worked with.

"I'll be the one working with him, but sometimes it helps to have the name of the actual attorney with McDaniel."

I left her to her work and headed out to my car. Time to see if I could find the truck that had been in the parking lot last night.

Chapter Seventeen

I parked by the grocery store in town. The dojo's parking area was blocked by orange cones and the door itself had yellow crime scene tape. It didn't appear that anyone had tried to tear it down yet. Cars slowed down as they drove by, looking at the building, perhaps wondering what had happened, or more likely, someone in the car was taking a photograph of the building as it stood now. The grapevine in a small town was fast and I had no doubt that everyone knew about the death.

The grocery store was quieter than when I normally did my shopping. I considered changing my hours so I could come mid-morning in the middle of the week. I walked down the sidewalk, which, while there were a few people going in and out of the grocery store, was empty of other foot traffic.

Not many people walked around the corner. There would be a handful of people out and about on the main street. I stared across the way at the dojo, hoping to make out any trucks but the one from the other night had the good sense not to show up for me.

A car honked around the corner, probably at someone who had stopped to get a parking space in front of the place they planned to visit. Probably not stopping for lunch as it was a little early for that, so maybe the laundromat or perhaps one of the little shops like the Cornered Reader.

Bill was sitting in the window, looking at a book. He noticed me walking and waved. I decided that perhaps he had some ideas about Dale. Clay certainly had them.

A bell over the door sounded as I walked in. Clay looked up from where he was talking to another customer, a rather short, thin young man who was talking earnestly to him about something. His voice was low and between that and the music I couldn't make out the words.

Clay had added a basket of soaps near the door and I picked out the fragrance of lavender over the aroma of books and wood. I passed it and sat down in one of the club chairs next to Bill. A small round table sat between us, books piled haphazardly on it. I figured Clay left those so people would know they could leave out books they were looking at and not return them to the wrong shelves.

The chairs were low enough that my feet touched the wood floor even when I leaned back against the blue fabric. The picture window had shelves up to the wide sill. The sill itself was where Clay displayed his new books. I knew he'd been planning a local authors window display but it wasn't there, probably because of Lily.

"How are you?" I asked Bill.

He chuckled. "Can't get much better than dead, can you?" Bill said.

I grinned. He always had a good attitude about being dead, at least I thought so.

"And you?" Bill asked. "Is that stupid girl still trying to get money out of Olive's books?"

"She got an attorney and he called," I said. "I contacted Ari Bowman and she gave me the name an attorney at the firm they use."

"Good. The Bowmans can be difficult but, overall, I think they're good people, for all they live up in New York mostly."

The Bowmans I worked with were scattered, though three of them still lived in New York City. The rest were all over the place and exactly where sometimes changed.

"They are," I agreed.

"Heard that Dale Benton was murdered," Bill said. "Also heard that the police are looking at the owner of the dojo. Don't you work out over there?"

"I do," I said. "It's hard to think that Brett would have done such a thing. And then to leave the body in the building."

I wasn't sure which was harder to fathom. Brett as a killer or Brett being so sloppy that he'd leave the body in the women's locker room. He was quite intense about making sure things were done just so in his business.

Bill nodded.

"Dale could get under your skin, though," he said finally. "He was a brat when he was stuck with his mom when she'd come in here. Run through the store screaming at the top of his lungs. I guess he did that a few times at the library, too. Ms. West wouldn't stand for it and Mrs. Benton was asked not to bring him back until he could behave."

Bill was clearly enjoying reminiscing. I wasn't about to stop him in case he shed some light on what was going on.

"After that, she'd look for reading materials here. We didn't want him either and I asked her to not come with him as he was making the other patrons uncomfortable. Mrs.

Benton was embarrassed by that, I can tell you, and after that she left him home. I heard he wasn't any better in school, either. Quite a handful."

"I doubt anyone murdered him because he was a wild kid." I mean, Dale wasn't all that young any more. I knew very little about him and what I did know seemed to be that Bill and Clay didn't like him. I wondered if that was generally true. I hadn't really talked to Mark like I'd planned, or Suzanne. And here I'd had both of them available at the hotel. Maybe this afternoon.

Bill gave me a half smile. "No, I doubt that. But Dale wasn't any better as an adult, either. He might not run through stores, but he didn't exactly play nice, if you know what I mean."

"I'm not sure," I said, hoping Bill would elaborate.

"He didn't come in here much as an adult, and by that time, I was limited in where I could go. Still, I heard things. I guess he didn't like taking no for an answer at the bar, particularly not from women. I don't think he ever went farther than being an annoyance, but it's not like people come to confide in me or anything."

I nodded at Bill.

"He could only get temp work because he wasn't trustworthy. Things went missing when he was around. He always had a scam. The one time he did come in, he was trying to get Clay to get in on some investment he had going, but Clay isn't one for risk taking so Dale left."

Clay hadn't mentioned that part.

"How long ago was that?" I asked.

Bill shrugged. "Don't know. Wasn't paying that much attention. I think it was spring, but whether it was this spring or last spring, I don't know. I just remember enjoying watching the people outside and everyone was mostly in shirt sleeves."

Which could about any time that it wasn't snowing. At least we'd ruled out winter, mostly, and probably the height of summer. In mid-summer we had days of it being quite hot but other days it was comfortable, particularly in the morning, although I would have thought Bill would have noticed short pants as well as the shirt sleeves. So probably either spring, early summer, or earlier this fall. We'd had a fairly warm July and August so most people would have been in shorts or maybe skirts.

If it were last year, that made things even more difficult considering we'd had a rather cool summer. I bit back a sigh, not wanting Bill to think I didn't find him helpful. I really did. And I appreciated him talking to me.

"Hard to keep track of time when you're dead," Bill said. "It's not like my days will ever be all that different. I just sit here and watch. Sometimes, when Clay isn't around, I'll wander around the store, but he's worried that if I wander up to someone and they get too cold, they'll get scared or something. I try to keep my wanderings to when the store is closed. There's a nice window upstairs that gives me a different view."

I nodded along, though I didn't really agree with Clay. If Bill wanted to wander, he ought to wander. Olive certainly hadn't caused any issues with the hotel.

"I was here because I was looking around for the truck I saw in the parking lot the other evening, the evening I found Dale," I said.

"Wasn't it his?" Bill asked.

"I don't know. It was there when I got there but gone when I came out after I called the police."

"What'd it look like? I might have seen it."

I described it to Bill as well as I could. Of course, without a color, no doubt he'd seen plenty of trucks going back and forth outside the window.

"There are three dark blue that have kind of a two-tone that drive up and down the street regularly," he said. "There's a brown two-tone that's old, more of a clunker. A newer brownish one, maybe more bronze, I guess. Those are the regulars that I see all the time. There are others I've noticed but they're not local, or at least don't drive like locals."

I knew what Bill meant. The locals knew where parking was so they'd head right to where they wanted to go. Non-locals often cruised slowly up the street looking around, hoping to see something near where they were headed. Locals always used the parking areas either at the grocery store or in the public parking behind the library down the way. Both were around the corner.

Locals also didn't tailgate along this street. Too many people stopping suddenly when they noticed a potential parking space opening up. That wasn't a hard and fast rule, of course, nothing was, but it was a tendency.

"That's helpful," I said. "Do you know if any are owned by guys who would do demo work?"

Bill shook his head. "Clay might know because he used to hang with some of the guys who went into construction. I think that's what he really wanted to do, work with his hands rather than working behind a counter, but he does good here. Still, he's inclined to believe the story about the dojo owner, Brett, rather than one of the demo guys."

"Do you think Brett did it?"

"He's come in here a few times and looked around. Seems like an easy going type. Can't see him getting so bent out of shape over someone stealing things from a locker than he'd kill someone. Course, running a dojo, he probably has the skill." Bill gave me a long stare.

Much as I hated to admit it, he was right about that. And he had reaffirmed what I thought about Brett. I really hoped he wasn't the one who had done it.

Chapter Eighteen

The bell over the door rang as more people came into the store while I was talking to Bill. No one really acknowledged us, perhaps thinking that we were just an older couple resting. There were more questions for Clay. He was going to be busy that day, so I probably ought to return later.

"I should get going," I said. "I mostly came to ask Clay what he knew about the other guys doing construction. And then to drive around and see what trucks I could find. I was hoping that maybe I'd see one that looked like the one I saw. At least that might give me a color."

Not that I could do anything with that information. I wasn't a detective and didn't have any access to the information in the vehicle licensing records. But I would know.

"Clay likes the construction crew," Bill said. "I doubt he'd say anything bad about any of them, or even something that could be construed as bad. And he didn't like Brett."

"Really?" My hands had been on the arms of the club chair, readying to stand up, but now I relaxed them a little, though I was still sitting forward enough that my feet pressed down on the hardwood floor. It was the original floor to the store, that much I knew from Clay. It had taken time to sand down, refinish and polish, but now, it looked wonderful and gave the building character with the slight imperfections of the ancient wood.

Bill nodded. "Brett wasn't from around here, of course, but as I said he came in the store. I think he might have made a pass at Clay which made Clay uncomfortable."

I knew that Brett was gay but so far as I knew, Clay wasn't. He wasn't married or anything so maybe he just wasn't out.

"Just that?" I asked.

Bill sighed. "Clay thinks Brett may have asked around town in the wrong places about whether he—Clay--was gay or not. He's not. Just more, what do they call it now? Asexual? Or whatever." Bill paused looking down at his hands. "But it embarrassed him and he didn't like that, so he's inclined to believe the worst of Brett, even though it seemed like it was all a misunderstanding. Clay got laughed at by some of his buddies, the ones in construction, too, which made things worse."

"Was Dale involved?" I asked.

Bill shrugged.

He didn't seem to realize that potentially that could have given Clay a motive for murder.

"When did this all happen?"

"Shortly after Brett set up the dojo," Bill said.

Which meant it was less of a motive, unless something had happened more recently. I was inclined to doubt that. I didn't want to think that Clay could have done such a thing any more than I wanted to believe Brett could have.

"I've probably said too much," Bill said. "But now I care so little about things most people keep personal that I get carried away. After all, there's not much personal in the afterlife."

I had a feeling Olive would argue that.

"Thanks for the information," I said. This time, I did stand. I glanced down at the pile of books on the table but nothing caught my eye. I slipped away from the chairs and glanced around at the books Clay was advertising. There was the local author table without Olive's book because he'd had to put that behind the counter. I did see it displayed behind the counter on a shelf. Perhaps readers purchasing other things would see it and get excited about it.

Lily hadn't done herself any favors tearing up the books if she really wanted some royalties. She'd probably just kept us from selling as many copies as we could have.

The bell rang when I left the store, pausing to let a young woman in. I hurried out onto the street. I decided to walk down the main street first. There weren't a lot of people out, but enough that the streets weren't empty. Some of the people were dressed in outdoor wear that looked new. Probably tourists. I recognized the older couple that I thought were here to see leaves. There were more people that I didn't recognize.

We weren't the only hotel around and we were full with the vampire conference. I smiled at a couple of girls walking towards me so I had to avoid rolling my eyes at the thought of the conference. I'd rather have had the people looking at leaves.

The breeze that blew down through the town was cool as I walked along the sidewalks. The shops around me were all older brick buildings, most with narrow windows on either side of the door. The buildings had all originally been narrow, like rowhouses, rather than the wider buildings we had now. I got to the next cross street where I could see the police station. Behind it, facing the other direction, though they shared a parking lot, was the courthouse, a rather stately white building with stairs that rose up well above my head. They were so steep and tall that they couldn't build a long enough ramp. Instead, there was a side door for accessibility and an elevator that took people up to the upper floors.

On the occasions I'd had to go there, I'd used the elevators. Considering the wait times, it seemed everyone else did as well.

Down the next block was Carmichael's, which was wider than most of the buildings. There were stairs down to a basement there where they had a bar with music. Neither the restaurant nor the bar was open just yet.

The cars on the street were mostly SUVs and some sedans. I didn't see anything that looked like the truck I had seen. The single truck parked across the way was bright red, which I knew wasn't the truck in the dojo parking area.

A particularly strong breeze hit and I decided to turn back. I was cold and wasn't learning anything on my walk. Driving, I could at least go further out of town and maybe see a truck that struck a cord parked at a house somewhere. Of course, walking back to my car in the grocery store lot, I couldn't help but think that that was like looking for a needle in a haystack. I didn't even know for sure that the person with the truck even lived locally. This was a foolish errand.

I was shivering by the time I got back to my car. Bill wasn't in his chair by the window when I passed the bookstore. I wondered where he'd wandered off to. He didn't normally do that. I glanced up and noticed that he was standing at the upper window on the side of the building, looking out. Clay wouldn't like that, lest Bill have startled someone, but perhaps Clay was too busy to care. It was just unfortunate that Bill hadn't been standing there the other night. He might have seen something.

The grocery store lot was mostly empty. A single black truck was parked there but it didn't look the way I remembered the truck from the dojo. That truck had been smaller than the way this one looked. And this one was shinier, though it was dirty and muddy. Of course, I couldn't be certain that I'd have noticed the differences in the dark. The mud made me wonder if perhaps the lower part of the two-tone was just dirt. The truck had been far away.

Looking for a specific truck wasn't just looking for a needle in a haystack, it was searching for something like a needle when I wasn't even exactly sure what thing looked like.

Sighing, I got into my car. As I turned the key and waited for the interior to heat up, I thought about whether I wanted to go back to the hotel to talk to Suzanne and Mark about Dale or if I wanted to continue my search for the truck. If I headed back, I could also talk to Dori, which I hadn't done. I wondered what she thought about Brett being a suspect in the murder. She worked at the dojo teaching her own classes. She'd know him.

That decided me. I drove out of the lot and back towards the resort. Traffic was heavier going out of town than into it. The main road out to the resort was the highway into Tennessee. That didn't mean it was busy as in stop and go. Most people who were going a long distance went over the mountains by Asheville. The highway there was more direct and a bit wider. This road was for the people in the northern part of the state heading to Johnson City or thereabouts.

A dark blue and silver truck, not so shiny raced by me in

the left lane. It caught my eye because it looked like the truck that I had seen in the parking lot. It might not be the exact truck, but I wanted to know the make and model and maybe even the year, if I could find that out.

It was well past my exit by the time I had registered it, so I turned off and headed to the hotel. It probably wasn't the same truck and if it was, I had no desire to drive over the state line to Tennessee just to see if I could catch up to it and try and identify the make. My luck, speeding like that, I'd get a ticket and have no more information to show for my efforts. At least at the hotel, I could commiserate with people I knew.

Chapter Nineteen

After I arrived and parked in the garage below the restaurant, I walked up the stairs to the main part of the steakhouse. The restaurant was joined only by the underground tunnel and a covered walkway from the hotel. It allowed people to charge items to their rooms but it wasn't in our main building.

Nominally, I was their boss, though the head chef had an administrative person that did most scheduling, and the chef herself did the food ordering. I rarely, if ever, suggested any changes to the orders. I looked them over because that was my job, but I trusted that she knew what she was doing.

Dori worked in the kitchen as a sous chef. She had Mondays off when she taught her classes at the dojo. It was early enough that while she'd be working, but she wouldn't be so busy that she couldn't chat with me if I didn't interrupt her slicing and dicing. She tended to prefer to be on that table and she was good with a knife.

I shuddered at the thought, suddenly glad that the man in the dojo had been bludgeoned. While Dori could probably have done that given her martial arts background, at least people didn't immediately think of her when they thought of knife work.

The kitchen music was louder than that of the bar. Workers talked and yelled across the room. Everyone was busy at their stations. Even the servers were coming in and getting ready to go out for the lunch crowd, though we were not yet open. Someone was probably doing a last pass to make sure tables were clean and ready for customers.

"Morning," I said, raising my voice slightly to catch Dori's attention. Her station was a place with a large counter so she could chop. The stainless-steel shelving below gleamed in the harsh lights and the white tile floor was spotless. I knew that any time someone dropped something there was a person to clean it up before anyone stepped or possibly slipped on it.

"Morning," Dori said. She didn't take her eyes off the onions she was chopping. I found the work fascinating, the way the knife came up most of the way and she pushed the onion a fraction further under it and then chopped down. Once done, she turned the pieces around and chopped them in the other direction, quickly and efficiently. It was hypnotic.

"I heard that the police are questioning Brett about the murder."

It could have been my imagination, but it seemed as if the knife was chopping a bit harder against the chopping board under the onion. A few pieces scattered about.

Dori paused and looked up at me. Her eyes were dry, though mine were getting a bit wet thanks to the onion chopping.

"It's ridiculous," she said. "Brett left with most of the demo guys. He didn't even know that there was anyone still there. He swears Dale was with them."

Dale must have gone back to the dojo then. I wondered why.

"I wonder why Dale went back to the dojo," I said. "And who knew in order to murder him?"

Dori shook her head.

"I haven't had run ins with him, but there are rumors. My girlfriend is from here and she said that Dale has always been something of a trouble maker. She thinks he was probably stealing something or thought there was something to steal."

"I heard that rumor. The one I heard was that Brett caught him stealing things out of the lockers as he removed them," I said. I should talk to Brett about the stuff in my locker.

"They had already cleared them out. Brett has all of the stuff in labeled bags for people. A lot of folks left things. I mean, it wasn't like we let people go into the locker rooms when we found out we were going to have to demolish the place. There were plenty of changes of clothing, some fitness trackers, deodorant, shampoo, and the like."

"I left some clothing in mine," I said. "And deodorant, although I care less about that."

"Brett will have it for you," Dori said. "He's good about that."

"I have a hard time seeing him as a murderer," I said. "I know someone was at the dojo when I went in. There was a truck in the parking lot. It was gone when I came out after the police got there."

Dori leaned back, clearly interested. "Do the police know? Brett doesn't drive a truck. If someone was there..."

"I told them. I even went into town to see if I could find a truck that looks like it. Of course, that was like searching for a needle in a haystack."

"At least you tried. It's more than I can say I did. I was just here working. And when they asked me, I had nothing to add. I met the demo guys, including Dale, before I left but I didn't know any of them. My girlfriend is younger than most of them so she didn't know them well, but her older brother was in their group for a bit, until he moved down to Charlotte and got a job there. More building, I guess, but he comes home on holidays."

"I can't say that looking for a truck was worth my time. I talked to Bill and Clay at the bookstore. They didn't really know anything."

"Clay hates Brett. He says it's because Brett made a pass at him, but Brett really just wanted to know more about the bookstore and setting up a business in Glade Springs," Dori said. "It was a huge misunderstanding, but between Clay's acting all insulted and the fact that he told the construction guys about it, it's become this thing. And Clay is embarrassed that people know he got propositioned by a guy."

"Bill mentioned something about that," I told her.

Dori shivered as if she wasn't at all interested in talking to a ghost. I didn't really understand the sentiment because she was never bothered by Olive.

"I hope that the detectives get their heads out and find the real culprit. I mean, even Clay has as much reason to kill Dale as Brett. Dale was the one guy who kept the joke about Brett propositioning Clay alive. I guess that was par for the course, but still. Brett didn't really care. He's definitely out of the closet, but Clay may not be."

I didn't add that Bill thought his son was just asexual, because it wasn't important. Nor did I want to get into an argument about it.

"I wish we knew who did do it."

"If it's someone with a truck, I'd look at Teena Anderson," Dori said. "She used to date Dale. She was also hoping to date Brett but, well, that's never going to happen. Still, she has a hard time taking no for an answer."

"But why kill Dale now? Did they just break up?" I asked.

Dori shook her head. "That was a long time ago. Dale is a jerk, though, so who knows what he might have done. And Teena holds a grudge."

I wasn't sure that Teena, who was a slight thing with bleached blonde hair and breasts of a size and perfect shape that didn't look quite natural on the rest of her figure, had the strength to bludgeon someone to death. But she was in my class. Not my favorite person and I knew that she knew a lot of people, or rather men. She ignored women, mostly. If anyone could persuade someone else to do something for them, it was Teena.

At least I'd learned something I could use. And I knew that someone else didn't believe Brett was a killer. Of course, Dori had thrown as much suspicion on Clay as on Brett. I hoped it wasn't Clay, either.

Dori and I talked for a bit longer, but the kitchen was getting busier and she'd slowed down her chopping. I left her to her work and walked back down the hallway to the main part of the hotel. I could live with Teena being the one who killed Dale but, unfortunately, she didn't seem like she could have done it. Besides, even if Dale was a jerk as Dori said, I highly doubted that she would have killed him simply because they had once been a couple. That didn't mean that she couldn't have another motive that I didn't know about.

Also, if Teena had hired someone, then there was the need to find her motive and who she might have hired. Sighing, I shook my head. Solving mysteries was far more difficult than running a resort hotel. At least when things didn't go the way they should at the hotel, I could fix them. Plus, the only times I'd been in any real danger in the hotel were the times I was investigating a murder.

Back in the main part of the hotel, I noticed the crowd of people all in black milling around. From what I heard, people were grumbling. I started to walk past them when one of the young women who had reported Logan missing to us yelled out. "Hey! That's the hotel manager who wouldn't do anything!"

Suddenly everyone in their black outfits turned to look at me. I swallowed hard hoping that none of them would actually bite. It was a vampire conference, after all.

Chapter Twenty

I froze, suddenly worried about what would happen as the group in black stared at me. The doors to the conference room were open, the windows showing the clouds outside that were clearing slightly, though even between the clouds themselves, the sky was a blue so pale it might have been colorless. The room suddenly felt too warm and the bodies pressing closer stank as if water was a bigger anathema to vampires than sunlight.

"What's the problem?" I asked kindly, hoping to diffuse the situation.

I knew that our security monitored the cameras, though they might miss certain things. Hopefully me being surrounded by a bunch of young people who dressed like vampires would have someone walking in to investigate in the not-too-distant future. I could only hope that it happened before the group jumped me and maybe started draining my blood.

"You know very well." The taller of the young women I had met with earlier stomped closer to me, bringing her face up to mine. "We need to find Logan Fulton and you wouldn't look for him."

"I opened his room. He wasn't in there. I can't go through the entire hotel," I explained. "That would be an invasion of privacy of our other guests."

"That makes you an accessory to a kidnapping!" the woman practically screamed at me.

"The police have different abilities, which is why I insisted you call them," I reminded her.

"Fat lot of good that did," someone else said. "Logan still isn't around. He could be anywhere, but no one will look for him!"

The group started chanting something though I couldn't make out the words. There were at least three bodies between me and the stairs. There were people behind me so I couldn't slip back down the hallway. Not that I wanted to be seen running away from the crowd. Even so, I was terribly uncomfortable.

The room chilled. I half expected to see Clara running down the hallway, passing through the people unfortunate enough to be standing in her path, but instead Olive wandered in from the main conference room. She strolled over to me, slipping between people, though I have to admit that sometimes her shoulder would pass through another body. I wondered what that felt like to her. I knew that for the human it would feel as if a block of ice had just hit them.

One young person, probably a young man, though I couldn't be certain, rubbed his shoulder through his black cape.

"Maggie!" Olive said when she got closer. "I'm so glad I found you. I really do need to chat with you upstairs." She turned to the people standing between me and the stairs and paused as if she couldn't just walk right through them. I wondered what the crowd would do if she did.

"She's talking to us," the girl who seemed to be the ring leader snapped.

"I believe she's needed at the desk. They've found something to do with one of the guests and the police are there," Olive said.

Most of the crowd surged up the stairs. I was just out of the way enough that I wasn't completely pushed along.

"Did you have to say something?" I muttered, thinking about having to push through the crowd to get to the police.

"Let's head to the elevators," Olive suggested and drifted that way. Really, when she'd appeared to stroll, she'd been drifting. Her feet never quite touch the ground.

I followed, pressing the button for the next floor. I had no idea who was looking into Logan's disappearance. I hoped that I'd be able to push my way in so I could talk to them.

Once inside the elevator, Olive chuckled. "I lied. The police aren't here. But they seemed to want to know something from you. I figured that saying something was happening would get you out of the crowd."

She looked at me, a smug smile on her face, waiting for me to applaud her quick thinking.

"I thought you couldn't hear what was going on if you aren't visible," I said.

"I can't. I saw the crowd and waited in the conference room. I heard them talk about not finding Logan so I came out and suggested that the police were there."

"They aren't going to be happy," I said as the doors opened to the lobby, which was now crowded with people in black.

"No, but they'll be unhappy in an area where more staff

are around. And I won't be." Olive wiggled her fingers at me in goodbye before she popped out.

Stepping off the elevator, taking in the problem I had now, I noticed that the crowd spilled around the fireplace and the main desk. Plenty of people stood on the stairs trying to see what was going on, though I knew they had very little ability to do so. A few of them went back down to the basement.

It made me wonder if any of the speakers had shown up.

I kept my head down and pushed my way to the desk, slipping in behind it.

"Where are the cops? Did you send that woman to lie to us?" the tall girl naturally spotted me. I wondered if she were related to Lily, who also seemed eager to yell at me for things that I couldn't control.

"Like you, I thought the police were here. Olive just told me it was a ruse," I explained. "However, I'd like to know if any of your speakers have turned up."

"What's it to you?" one of the young men asked. He had a patchy beard that reminded me of a calico cat for some reason. Some of his hairs were darker than others and his pale white skin gave rise to yet a third color of his beard.

"It suggests to me that perhaps Logan wasn't doing what you expected him to do, which is another thing the police ought to be aware of," I said. I turned before they could yell anything at me and entered my office. I hated leaving Mark and Suzanne with the rather angry crowd, but I wanted to call Sissy and see if she knew anything more.

Sissy picked up after only a single ring.

"What's up?" she asked. "I haven't been able to get ahold of Logan if that's what you're calling about."

I told her the concerns of the people out at the front desk.

"I wish I could be more help. I tried calling the number listed on the website when I couldn't get Logan, but no one answers and the voicemail is full," Sissy said. "Hospitality has told me that the conference goers are getting restless and there were a bunch of complaints about the food, which should have gone to someone in charge, but there's no one really in charge."

"What sort of complaints?" I asked, hating to think that we were letting people down in that area as well.

"The usual," Sissy said. "They didn't like the chicken because it was too dry or not flavorful enough. One person didn't get the vegetarian meal they had reserved until most of the other people at their table had finished. We worked with them on that one because that was our fault, though it would have helped to have an organizer to talk with as well."

It made me feel better that most of the things were taste things and not something my staff was doing wrong.

"I've gotten messages about speakers not arriving but that's not something I can help with. Logan didn't give me a list, nor were they comped anything through the hotel, though I would have made sure they at least got a ticket for a free drink or something if the organizer had asked." Sissy sounded put out.

"Basically, we have a bunch of people here for a conference and they're all on their own," I summarized.

"It sounds like it," Sissy agreed. "I wish I could be more help."

Sighing, I hung up the phone. I wished I could be of more help considering how many people expected me to be.

I heard grumbles from out front and someone was loudly saying "Excuse me," over and over on repeat. They didn't sound pleased. I was unsurprised to see Detective Granger standing at the front desk.

My day was just going from bad to worse.

Chapter Twenty-One

I felt a headache threatening, though fortunately it wasn't quite there just yet. The crowd was all talking at once and from my partially hidden vantage point it appeared that Granger was the person they were focused on. Maybe the woman who was yelling at me recognized Granger as a police officer or perhaps it was the harsh way Granger had screamed "Excuse me" to push her way to the desk.

At any rate, I was thankful that someone else was taking the heat from the conference goers. I could use the break.

Of course, the phone on my desk rang just then. I glared at it for a second before picking it up.

It was the paralegal from the attorney's office.

"I wanted to give you a head's up. McDaniel wasn't pleased to hear from me and after a brief chat, he'll be chatting with Ms. Campbell about the lawsuit. It seems that my brief showing that names weren't protected unless Olive Hughes had created a trademark got to him. Also, Olive's not a famous author herself, so there's really nothing that can be done. While it's questionable that you made the decision to use her name—although Ms. Bowman said there were *reasons*—there's nothing Ms. Campbell can do about it. If she complains further and McDaniel contacts me again, I'll let you know."

I debated telling her about Lily defacing books in the Cornered Reader but decided that was up to Clay to do. Instead, I thanked her and hung up. Now I could just hope that I didn't run into Lily Campbell around the hotel. It was ironic that I had this person acting like a financial vampire at the same time we had a group of vampire lovers. And none of them were pleased with me.

Mark walked into the office and stared at me for a moment not saying anything. He took a breath, let it out, clearly trying to figure out how to say what he wanted.

"What is it?" I asked.

"Detective Granger is here. And the people at the front desk are angry that you're back here and they want to talk to you, or rather, I guess yell at you, although for what I'm not quite certain. Granger seems to think the missing conference organizer is your problem as well," Mark said. He sighed and looked at me pityingly.

I stood up frowning.

I went up to the desk. The chants of wanting to find Logan got louder.

"What are you doing about it?" the tall woman demanded.

"I'm talking to the detective," I said sweetly. "Perhaps if you all spoke nicely, she'd listen?"

Granger glared at me even harder than her usual stare.

"I'm actually here to speak to you about another guest. Is there a place that's less busy?" she asked.

I went around and gestured to her to come back to sit in my office. It wasn't like Granger didn't know exactly where my office was and how to get there. She'd made herself at home there before.

"Rory Ingles," Granger said.

"What about him?" I asked.

"You texted Ed that he'd had an altercation with the missing conference organizer. We're looking for him because he spoke with the deceased man that you found in the dojo when you claimed you were looking for clothing you left behind," Granger said.

It wasn't lost on me how she used the word claimed, as if I hadn't actually been looking for clothing when I found the dead man.

"It seemed relevant," I said.

"Yet you said that you'd never met the deceased before."

"I hadn't," I said.

"But you knew that we wanted to talk to Rory Ingles?" Granger pressed.

"You came into the hotel asking for him," I said. "The name stood out. And there was another woman who had the same last name who checked in that evening with a conference discount on the room and then left around midnight the same night. Which is unusual. It's not like she could fly home that same day and it doesn't take that long to drive to Charlotte. We had her down as being from further away."

"We have witnesses claiming that Dale Benton and Rory Ingles met in town around the time you claim to have talked to Brett Evans with the rest of the class in the dojo. They were seen arguing. Did you notice Mr. Ingles when you returned after dark to the closed business and entered without permission?" Granger asked.

When she put it like that, it did sound like I'd done

something wrong. Of course, Brett wouldn't have cared, unless of course he'd been the one to murder Dale.

The edges of the headache became a full-blown headache. I sighed.

"And?" I asked.

"You didn't see anyone there?" Granger pressed again.

"I told you. I went in. I heard someone go through the door as I was on the phone with 911. I thought they were entering but no one came into the locker room. When I'd arrived, I noticed a truck around back. I thought that perhaps everyone had gone to dinner and one was left behind. I almost didn't try the door but when I did, it was unlocked."

Everything I said was true, though it was scattered.

"The truck was gone when I left."

"Which you conveniently can't describe better than 'a truck'," Granger repeated.

I sighed.

"What exactly is it you want from me?" I asked.

"I want to know if you know more than you're letting on considering how you've involved yourself in our other investigations. Having to help solve a murder when there are no police available due to a storm is different than when we are available. Inserting yourself into something that became a murder isn't okay and could mess up our case, particularly if you aren't being forthcoming."

"I have no idea what you think I was inserting myself into. I wanted my clothing. I should have called Brett, but it didn't occur to me that he'd be available to the phone. It seemed just as easy to run into town and talk to him there, at the dojo. I had no idea that the men he'd hired to clear the place out would do it so quickly. In fact, if he hadn't been planning to have it torn down, I'd have expected the place to be open when I arrived," I said.

"In addition, I told you everything I know, even things I wasn't certain you'd care to know by sending texts about information I had because I work in a hotel where people are. The fact that one of your suspects had an altercation with another person that has gone missing seemed like the kind of thing you'd want to know. I know that because one of the women reporting Logan's disappearance told me. It was one reason they were concerned about Logan."

"Because he'd argued with Rory Ingles?" Granger clarified.

I nodded.

"And you think, what...that Ingles is here on a murder spree?"

"I have no idea. It just seemed like the kind of information you might want to know. As you keep pointing out, I'm not a detective."

Granger stared at me.

"I think you might want to contact missing persons about your conference organizer. I work homicides," Granger said standing up. Unfortunately for her, she was so short that standing up didn't give her any extra height. Still, she held her head high as she marched out of my office. She ignored the people at the desk who were still trying to get some attention.

I picked up the phone to call Lyle.

Chapter Twenty-Two

I hit Lyle's number on my cell, staring out at the front desk from the safety of my little office. Some of the people had left but the woman who was most vocal about finding Logan was still there. I ignored her. I had no doubt someone had told her to contact missing persons already. I didn't need to go out and get yelled at for passing on information. It wasn't as if I had the authority to do anything more than I had already done.

I had, in fact, done more. Olive was out looking for the young man or at the very least keeping an eye out. So far, she hadn't reported finding him, which was a little strange. Normally she could breeze through the hotel quite quickly, but perhaps she had to look at people a little closer since she'd never seen the young man in person.

Pizza smells mixed with French fries and a floral perfume that someone had on far too much of, which surprised me given that the people outside the desk were mostly young people dressed in black, reached me. From everything I'd read, vampires tended to have a heightened sense of smell so I would have guessed vampire lovers would wear less scent to be more enticing. Of course, assuming that vampire lovers at a conference would think logically was probably a stretch.

I looked down at the dark screen of my computer, which dared me to move the mouse and wake it up while I waited for Lyle to answer. I glared at the monitor, daring it to wake up without my touch. I was not in a good mood. Lately it seemed as if people expected things of me that it wasn't possible to give. I was being blamed for things I had no control over. As if it were my fault I had found a dead body, had to sign books with Olive's name, and had a conference organizer go missing. The last was the one that was closest to actually being my fault, but it really was out of my control.

"What's going on?" Lyle asked. Wind whistled around him.

"Are you driving?" I asked when it paused and I heard the rumble of a motor.

"Stopped now," he said. "I'm on hands free."

"Of course you are," I said. "I'm just checking in to see if you'd heard anything else about Dale Benton's death. And, also, if you've picked up any chatter about our missing conference organizer."

"I got a call about half an hour ago from missing persons making sure that we hadn't had any cars in any of the parking lots left overnight," Lyle said. "Probably about your missing organizer. I haven't heard anything directly. Do you need me to look into it?"

A park ranger, Lyle was on good terms with the detectives and the police, something I wasn't. Or if I wasn't on their naughty list, I didn't know them well enough to ask things.

"I'm frustrated," I said.

I told him about the women who expected me to go through all the rooms. And that Detective Granger seemed to think there was something odd about me going into the dojo to retrieve my clothing.

"She made it sound like I was trespassing. There were no signs and it's a place that's normally open at that time. While I knew Brett was having it cleared out, I expected people to be there," I explained.

"I get it," Lyle said. "Al's probably after something, but it's not you. I think she might have been hoping that you knew Brett was around. They really do think he did it."

"I have a hard time believing it," I said. "He's so nice. And he cares about that place. I can't see him harming someone for stealing clothing."

"People can surprise us," Lyle said not willing to commit to supporting me but also not willing to anger me further by pressing for Brett's guilt.

"At least the paralegal that contacted the attorney about using Olive's name called and it sounds like she schooled him on whether or not there was a case."

"That's one headache off your plate," Lyle agreed. I heard beeping.

"I've got to go," he interjected. "Something has come up. I'll keep you posted if I hear anything about Dale or your missing organizer."

I hung up the phone feeling vaguely better. As I was about to get up and go to the desk, now that it was quieter, though several of the black-clad guests were milling about the reception area, drawing attention from our non-conference guests, the office got cold. Olive appeared.

"Did you find him?" I asked.

"I don't think he's here," she said. "I've been through all the rooms twice. I checked out all the public areas I can get to—you'll have to check the restaurant or ask Smithers, not that he's likely to tell you anything—and not seen that young man. I've brushed by most of the people in dark clothing in case he was disguising himself but I can't find him."

"That's weird," I said. "He's not checked out."

"It's possible he realized how angry people were with him and left for a time. He could be in town at the bar there. Or out hiking, but I don't see people who love vampires as being the sorts to enjoy nature when they're stressed. I picture them curling up in a closet with a round of garlic," Olive said.

I blinked, attempting to see if I agreed or not. Finally, I just gave a nod of my head. I didn't really see the vampire lovers as being stressed, but Olive was right. As a group, this didn't seem like the sort of group that would be out and about in nature.

"At least that means if something happened to him, it's not our fault," Olive said, "and the hotel won't get more bad publicity. I know you've marketed this as a haunted hotel but really, we need to stop having high profile deaths here. It's just not good for business."

As if I could single handedly stop people from being murdered. Of course, this was just another example of me being expected to do things that were not possible for me to do. Sighing, I attempted to not glare at Olive while I walked to the door to see what was happening.

"I did see one thing..." Olive added as I reached the door.

I looked back at her, raising an eyebrow.

"That young woman who's been at the desk?" Olive said.

I nodded knowing she meant the tall woman who had

reported Logan missing. "She's been talking to everyone. Plenty of whispering. Unfortunately, any time I appeared and got near, the whispers silenced. There's something going on and she knows what it is."

Interesting. That was worth knowing. If I were good, I'd report that to Detective Granger, or perhaps Detective Penn who I had a slightly better relationship with. I was not, however, good. It was completely possible that Granger would just get frustrated with me attempting to learn things. She had really set me in a no-win situation.

I'd pretend I didn't know anything about what the woman was doing and hope it had nothing to do with our missing person. Or anything else going on in town. Of course, I really ought to know better than to try and hide my head in the sand.

Chapter Twenty-Three

The tall, demanding woman glared at me as I walked out and went to ask Suzanne and Mark if they needed anything. I wasn't surprised that they didn't. A few of the black clad guests who were still up in the reception area were dancing around to the music we had playing. A couple of others had wandered into the bar. The woman glaring at me stood near the fireplace and had her arms crossed, staring at us, as if her very looks could convince me, or perhaps any one of us, to do something.

"I wanted to ask both of you about Dale Benton," I said. "I guess that Detective Granger thinks Brett could have murdered him."

Mark rolled his eyes.

"Dale was older than my sisters and me," Suzanne said quietly. "I sort of knew of him, I think everyone did, but I didn't really know him. My dad won't hire anyone who uses him as a sub, though. I was out of the house before I learned that. I think it was at Christmas or something that it got mentioned. I didn't ask further. I probably should have."

"Not your problem," I said. "It's not like we knew we'd want to know more about him."

"Dale hung with one of my cousins," Mark said. "They fell out a few years back, which was sort of Dale's thing. He'd fall out with people and then they'd forgive him or maybe forget about the falling out and they'd hang for a bit. He was like that with work, too. My cousin's comment was that he was surprised someone hadn't killed him before now."

"Does your cousin think Brett did it?" I asked.

Mark shrugged. "We hadn't heard the police were looking at anyone in particular, so I haven't asked. I suspect that Brett's not the only suspect, although he has the misfortunate to have been the person that owned the building where Dale was found."

"It sounds like Clay didn't like Brett much. Or Dale," I said.

"Richmond?" Suzanne asked.

I nodded.

"Yeah, there was that whole gay thing. That was kind of ongoing. I can't imagine Clay hurting anyone. He's always been quiet and non-confrontational. I think that's one reason why people just assume he's gay. Well, that and he's never really dated. No men. No women."

"Anyone know anything about Rory Ingles or where Dale might have met him?" I asked.

"Dale did work out of town," Mark said. "I mean people here wouldn't always hire him. And he always made sure he got publicity when he did something nice or good, so out of town folks wouldn't know what a jerk he was. They learned and I know he had to go further and further to get work sometimes. Late last summer, he worked on construction projects out in Hickory. He'd only been back a few weeks, I think."

"And then gets murdered. Do you suppose he could have done something there and they came here to kill him?" I asked. Dale must have worked on our grounds earlier in the summer, or maybe spring. I had just taken the detective's word for the fact that he'd been here. Not that that meant anything, really.

"How would they know where he was?" Suzanne asked.

I nodded.

"Rory Ingles isn't from Hickory, either," I said. "It's not like he was coming to see him from there."

"Back in the day, I think he did some training as an electrician," Suzanne said. "I think that's where my dad had the issue with him. He went out west to school there."

Nancy Ingles was from Las Vegas. If she and Rory were related, maybe Dale had dated her and they'd had a falling out. Or maybe he'd just borrowed money.

"But that was ages ago," Mark said. "Again, it's the sort of question of why now."

"Rory Ingles and Nancy Ingles were both from places west of here, are suddenly they're in town and at the hotel. Rory was supposed to meet with Dale, but he's disappeared, along with the conference organizer, who he was seen arguing with," I said. "Maybe it's all tied together."

"Logan was from Minneapolis, wasn't he? Not that far west," Suzanne said, smiling a little.

"He might not have been part of this but perhaps he's linked via Rory, who was at the conference. May he saw something or heard something and he's in hiding?" I suggested.

Just then my phone rang. Glancing down at the number I was surprised to see Lyle had called me back. I held up a finger and headed to my office to talk to him, again.

Chapter Twenty-Four

I considered closing the door, but wasn't up for the claustrophobia that came when I did that in the tiny office. I settled in my chair, knowing Suzanne and Mark wouldn't listen in. They'd probably continue discussing Dale and the missing conference organizer. I took a breath, immediately regretting it as the stink of cigarette smoke filled my nostrils.

Answering, I asked what had happened.

"I found your conference organizer," Lyle said.

"Is he okay?" I asked.

"We're heading into the park to find out where his friend Rory is. I guess they went hiking together and Rory went off trail for a second and Logan lost track of him. He's been in the woods most of the night and he looks it. Medics are on the way. He found his way out after attempting to search for his friend," Lyle said.

I sighed.

Lyle didn't have much more information, but I was thankful that Logan, at least, had been found. I set the phone down and wondered whether to tell the tall woman who was so insistent upon us finding Logan. I bit my lip as I thought about it.

While I wanted nothing more than to turn on my computer and get to work, I knew it would bother me if I didn't let the tall, annoying woman know that Logan had been found... and not on the property. I stepped out of the office. She still stood in the reception area, her arms crossed. She'd moved further from the fireplace, probably because she'd gotten too warm, and now stood in the middle of the reception area. A few other people walking through had to skirt around her. She acted like she didn't notice them.

When I gestured to her to come to the desk, she frowned. She glanced around making sure I wasn't talking to someone else before sauntering over as slowly as possible. It seemed as if she stepped in front of one old couple, purposely making their walk towards the door less direct. I regretted my impulsive kindness.

"What?" she demanded. "I have a right to stand there. And I can ask everyone if they've seen Logan since you won't do anything."

"I wanted to tell you that I had a call from the park service. A friend of mine works for them..."

"Bully for you. That has nothing to do with me."

"But it does," I said. "He found Logan off one of the hiking trails. I guess he and Rory got lost or something. Even if I had been able to search each room, I wouldn't have found him."

"He's staying in your hotel!" the woman snapped. "He's your responsibility."

"His room is my responsibility," I said, not caring to argue anything. "He was off our property. I am a hotel manager, not his mother."

I snapped at her a bit more than I normally would, but these people were getting ridiculous.

"I need to go find him. Where did you say he was?" the woman asked, not apologizing and continuing to glare at me.

"He's at one of the hiking trail starts. I'm not sure which one. I didn't ask that closely. However, the police are there because Rory Ingles is still missing."

The woman paled.

"If I can get your name, should the police come, I can have them call your room."

"That's okay," she said, turning and leaving.

She didn't look like the woman asking about Nancy earlier. I hadn't seen that person since. This woman also didn't seem like she *was* Nancy. It seemed strange that she hadn't been willing to give her name. I should have asked before going up to Logan's room. Maybe Addy had. I'd ask later when she came on duty.

I watched as she talked to a few other black clad people. A couple looked back at me, but mostly they hurried out towards the parking lot. Maybe they were going to drive around until they found the right trail. It wasn't my business. At least I knew where Logan was. Now I could only hope they found Rory and perhaps we'd get an answer about Nancy.

Mark looked over at me from where he was working. "She seemed a little strange."

"I can't believe she wasn't willing to even give me a first name," I said.

"Do you think she was in someone else's room and is worried we'll care?" Mark suggested.

"She's old enough to know that it's not likely to be a problem. At least I think so."

Mark nodded.

"This whole week is weird," Suzanne said. "Maybe it's all the vampire love folks or something."

"How are you and Olive doing on her newest book?" I asked, changing the subject.

"Olive finds the people in the basement distracting. She's still dictating, but not as much as usual, although the other night she was up for hours longer. Normally, conferences don't bother her, but these do. I've done some editing and there's more work on this one, as if she's losing her train of thought. Of course, I lose it sometimes with them. They scream at odd intervals and then there's a huge delay before people start laughing. I swear, something's going to happen and no one will notice."

"I haven't heard the screams up here," I said. Or in my apartment.

"I think, but I'm not sure, they're in one of the conference rooms," Suzanne said. "I have the far one that they aren't using and I hear it quite clearly. Olive is working down there as well so I expect she's hearing it, too. And she probably goes to check things out."

Olive would. She only had to pop out and poke her head through the wall to see what was happening. She only had to materialize if she wanted to listen in on a conversation.

"I'm surprised she hasn't told us what the screams are about," I said.

"Probably not something she cares to chat about," Suzanne said. "I mean, what if they're role-playing vampires and biting each other. Do you really see Olive coming and telling us that?"

I smiled at the thought. Olive would probably be scandalized if she saw them doing things like. She was very particular about not invading people's privacy. And it was the sort of thing she'd avoid talking about if she did see it.

The people dressed in black were all wandering around upstairs. I noticed another gaggle of them hurrying up from the basement.

"At least now, if she's working down there, the conference goers are all up here or are leaving the hotel," I said.

Mark frowned. "I can't imagine that they all suddenly know where to go."

We watched as the group sort of milled around outside. A few came back in, deciding it wasn't warm enough in the clothing they were wearing. A few of them were in light outfits, though most had capes. The day wasn't cold, but it was fall and the air was brisk and when the breeze came up it could be unexpectedly chill.

"I hope Rory's okay," I said. "I'd hate to have a guest die, even if they aren't in the hotel."

We chatted a bit. I was about to head back into the office when Lily marched up to the reception desk. She'd come from the direction of the elevators, though I couldn't see around the corner to be sure she'd not been lying in wait for me to let my guard down.

Standing at the desk, she glared at me.

"Can I help you?" Mark asked.

"I need to speak to her," Lily pointed at me.

Sighing, I went back over to the reception desk to see what it was she wanted now.

Chapter Twenty-Five

The bar music turned to an upbeat pop tune of the sort that made you want to dance. It was a poor background for getting yelled at by another guest. Not that I thought of Lily as a guest exactly. She was Olive's cousin.

Closer to the desk, I noticed the smell of alcohol on her breath. It wasn't that late in the day and this wasn't a bit of wine. This smelled like bourbon, which didn't seem like a typical afternoon drink. Afternoons were for sipping sangria, maybe a sweet drink with a cute name but not bourbon which always seemed to me more of a late evening or night drink. It needed to be savored in a large recliner in a study that smelled of a crackling fire and books.

"How can I help you?" I asked, though I really didn't think I could. Nor did I particularly want to know what she wanted.

"I want you to give me my fair share of the royalties," Lily demanded.

"I believe you have an attorney for that," I said.

"And he says I don't have a case, but I know I do. It's the right thing for you to do."

The air behind me got chill. I didn't turn.

"Suzanne has put in a lot of work which is why royalties go to a bank account she set up," I said. "And you had nothing to do with the writing."

"Olive was my cousin. And I loved her." Lily started to cry, as if that would change the laws and make us suddenly break down and give her something.

"Like you ever cared when I was alive," Olive snapped.

Olive leaned closer to me, practically brushing my shoulder which suddenly felt as if someone had rubbed a block of dry ice up against my skin. I shuddered a little. Olive moved a bit to the right, away from me. Suzanne cautiously stepped a bit further from her.

"This is ridiculous!" Lily practically screamed. A few people in the reception area turned to look. "You've made up someone to look like her! And where did you get her pearls! Those should have gone to me!"

Lily reached out to grab them, but her hand passed through Olive. Her fingers immediately got a little less pink.

She frowned.

"I'm not someone made up to look like me," Olive said. "I am me. And I'm a ghost. I wrote those novels, so the money goes where I want it to go. And I prefer that Suzanne take care of it. Maggie is my friend and she's signing for me as I can't hold a pen. It's one of the downsides of being dead. Not that it matters considering you didn't have time for me when I was alive. There are many things I have forgotten about my life, but the fact that you and your mother couldn't do the smallest things for me when I was going through my divorce is not one of them."

Olive looked close to tears at that. It wasn't a look I ever expected from her. She always seemed so in charge of her emotions. In some ways she seemed a bit above the emotional breakdowns so many of us were prone to.

Lily stared.

"I don't believe you. My cousin knew we all loved her. We were always there for her. Why when she got divorced, I called her daily."

"To berate me for getting a divorce," Olive snapped.

"As if you would know!" Lily said. "You might be made up to look like my cousin but you most certainly know nothing about her!"

"Oh piffle!" Olive said, straightening. She glided through the counter, coming so close to Lily that the poor woman had to be freezing. Lily took a single step backwards and her jaw tightened, probably to keep her teeth from chattering, but she said nothing.

"I remember when you were born. You had a pink rabbit that you'd never let go of. What was its name? Oh yes, Pinkie. Original." Olive stared at her.

Lily's mouth opened and closed.

"You probably read that somewhere."

"Where?" Olive asked. She moved closer.

Lily backed up again. Then she turned and hurried away. Olive sighed. She looked around. A few people in the reception area were watching.

Moving closer to the desk, Olive lowered her voice. "I hope I didn't scare anyone away. Except maybe Lily. Her, I don't care about."

The staring people started to go on about their day, one of them looking back at us and frowning slightly.

"I think they'll get over it," I said. "We are, after all, a haunted hotel. They have to expect the possibility of a ghost."

Chapter Twenty-Six

I heard nothing for the rest of the afternoon. After, I had a quiet evening with the cats. I heard no screams coming from the conference area, but then I hadn't heard anything before, either. If they were closer to where Olive and Suzanne were working, then they'd have had to be loud indeed for me to hear them.

Lyle didn't call to tell me anything else. I would have liked to have known he was back home and not walking around the forest in the middle of the night as part of search and rescue. I decided not to call, since I'd torment myself with worry if he didn't answer.

Despite the quiet evening, I had a restless night and was tired when I got up. The cats were clearly displeased with me as they weren't on the bed when I woke up but were out on the sofa. Chai glared at me when I came out to feed them. I must have moved around far too much.

After feeding them their canned food, I made my usual toast and coffee and sat down on the sofa to have my basic breakfast. My phone rang as I was finishing.

"This is Maggie," I said. The call was from the main desk and it was late enough that it was probably Suzanne.

"There are some people here from the conference. They're wondering about Logan," Suzanne said. "He's not answering the phone in his room and no one has been able to reach his cell phone."

I sighed.

"I know he was found near a hiking trail. Have they called the local hospital in case he was taken there?" I asked.

"They did. The hospital released him last night. They're worried something happened to him in his room."

Sighing and feeling a bit like I was in the movie Groundhog Day, I put my cup in the sink and headed upstairs. I'd go in and check his room to make sure there wasn't a body there. This time as I walked down the hallway, I noticed there weren't many people in the conference area and a staff member was vacuuming the rug. It looked as if the conference attendees had left quite a mess considering the number of trash bags sitting next to the wall.

"Has it been bad?" I asked, pausing.

The staff person, Cindi according to her name tag, nodded. "We've had three people cleaning up every morning. We've reported it to housekeeping. They ought to pay extra for the amount of garbage they leave around."

I'd definitely let Susie know, although I had a feeling my housekeeping manager would do the same. The more time people had to spend cleaning up downstairs, the slower they'd be cleaning rooms later on.

The music upstairs was a different tune than the last couple of days. The fire was already lit in the fireplace and the whole room felt homey. Outside it looked like rain and I hoped that Rory had been found.

The shorter of the two girls who had asked about Logan the other day was there. Her taller friend wasn't with her, for which I was glad.

"Are you certain Logan hasn't gone back out to the hiking trail?" I asked.

"He'd have answered his phone, don't you think?" the girl said, as sullen as her other friend was angry.

"There's not always coverage," I reminded her. "I can go up and check the room again."

The girl nodded, now happy that I was willing to go up and check the room. I made my way to the elevator while she trailed along behind. Part of me wanted to ask her for details, like a name and perhaps the name of her tall friend, but part of me wanted nothing to do with these people. The conference had started on Wednesday and was scheduled to go through Sunday. It was long for a fan conference, which was one reason Susie had been willing to work with them.

However, I was making a note that we weren't having them back at our hotel ever again.

The elevator smelled faintly of body odor. Normally our housekeeping staff is good about making sure the entire hotel smells fresh and clean. We have air filters to help but somehow this group had managed to make the elevator stink. Or perhaps it was just the person who had ridden down before I got in to ride up.

I knocked on Logan's door. Called out to him. No one came out of their room to complain this morning at least. Perhaps the person had checked out or they were part of the conference and weren't in bed yet.

Entering the room, I noticed the lights were on. Just about all of them. I placed my hand behind me to keep the young woman from running in. The bathroom was empty, though the towels were all over the floor, again. Considering he hadn't been around for people to find him, Logan was certainly good at throwing around our hotel towels.

I smelled the lemon scent of our cleanser over the stink of old socks that seemed to permeate everything. The bed was messed up as if someone had slept in it but no one was there. No body lay on the floor on the far side. I checked the closet and no one hid in there, afraid of vampires finding them.

Coming out, I closed the door and locked it. I considered turning off the lights but didn't want to disturb anything, just in case Logan turned up dead or injured somewhere and the room was a crime scene. It certainly looked like a crime scene for housekeeping.

"He's not there?" the girl whispered.

I shook my head. "He's been in the room since housekeeping was last here, so probably after the hospital, but it appears he's gone again."

She huffed and then marched off to the elevators. She swung her arms around and then turned to me.

"This conference is a nightmare. Logan isn't doing anything and hardly any of the speakers are here. Two of the ones who have shown up don't know where they're supposed to be and no one knows anything. We only got dinner because the hotel served it, but we had no speaker, other than some guy who stood up and started talking. Nancy Ingles was supposed to give the keynote about her new book coming out. I was really looking forward to it. She's been part of the vampire scene for ages and I was really proud of her for getting published."

I nodded. Interesting that Nancy wasn't just a guest,

she'd been a speaker and she'd left. I didn't share that detail with the girl.

We both took the elevator down. It was the same one, waiting for us, but at least the body odor smell had dissipated. While the guests here this week might not be great about hygiene, at least the air filters were working. Sighing, I thought that perhaps those were the only things that were.

Chapter Twenty-Seven

At least this morning I had had most of my coffee and hadn't been awakened early. However, my poor night's sleep meant I needed more caffeine. I headed towards the café, where a lot of our other guests were. I noted that the people in the café were mostly dressed in jeans and sweaters, ready for the weather. Only two people were dressed all in black as if they might be part of the vampire conference.

I waited in line and got my coffee after a few minutes. The guests ahead of me were talking about how rain was forecast and they needed to get their morning hike in before it happened. I wondered where they were going. It was such a nice normal conversation after everything I'd been involved in that I wished I could have stayed and listened to them longer.

Instead, I headed back to the desk. Suzanne was there. A small group of black clad guests were standing around talking to her. My stomach twisted. Not more complaints.

I walked around them, thankful that they were intent

upon their complaint and didn't notice me. I slipped in behind the desk and listened to what they were saying.

"But the rooms were non-refundable if there was a conference. There's been no conference," one of them was arguing.

"I'm sorry, but the terms were clear," Suzanne said. "I think you need to take it up with the conference organizers."

More arguing.

"What's going on?" I asked.

"The conference rate was a non-refundable rate after the first of this month," Suzanne said. "They want their money back for their stay here because there was no conference."

"If you check out today, we'll bill you for tonight but we can refund the next few nights," I said.

"That's bogus! We paid a lot of money to get here and then a ton of cash to stay here and you can only refund us for what we won't use? There wasn't even a conference! You ought to refund us that money as well!"

"We are not the conference," I said. "We're the hotel. We have expenses for the use of our facilities whether or not there's a conference. In a non-refundable situation, we normally wouldn't refund anything, however, I am willing to change that to a non-refundable 24-hour cancellation if you'd like. You'd get about half your stay credited."

"But then we wouldn't have a room, would we?" one of them asked. It was a young man this time. He looked as if he were too young to be traveling on his own, but I had noticed that as I aged, it became harder and harder to really tell the ages on younger people. For all I knew he could be nearly 30.

"No," I said. "You pay to stay here at the hotel. Everyone, even people who are not with the conference pay the hotel for a bed. That's how a hotel works."

"But this is a conference!" the guy argued.

"I can only refund the nights you don't use with 24 hours notice." I used my firm voice.

The three of them stepped away and started talking. One of them wanted to take the offer and go. The other was arguing for trying to get the money and then stay.

"There are cheaper hotels around," I said. I listed them and the towns they were in. All would require a car and a commute, but perhaps the prices would entice these people to leave. At this point, I didn't care that the hotel would lose money on the conference. I wanted it over.

A couple of them put their heads together.

"Yeah, then, we want to check out. How do we do that?"

"You turn in your keys and we'll start the paperwork," I explained.

"But how will we get our stuff?" one of them asked.

"You might want to do that first," I replied.

They left, hopefully to go do just that.

"Did you get their room number?" I asked Suzanne.

She nodded. "This has been a nightmare."

"You're telling me. I just learned that Nancy Ingles was a writer. She recently got a book published and she was supposed to give the speech during dinner."

"But she's the one who left, right?" Suzanne clarified.

I nodded.

"Weird."

Suzanne pulled out her phone and tapped in a few words.

"Okay, here she is. She's got a vampire romance book

published. It looks like every other vampire romance I've seen online."

"You read vampire romance?" I asked.

Suzanne laughed. "Not really, but I was teaching myself to recognize covers by genre so I could get a better feel for how Olive's book should look. I hired someone to do the cover quite reasonably, but I still needed to know what we wanted and I wanted to be sure to steer Olive in the right direction."

"Of course."

I left Suzanne to get back to her work and headed into my office. I'd use the large computer to look Nancy up. It seemed important that she was a major guest speaker that left. Perhaps she realized upon getting here just how poorly the conference was being run and got out before she had to deal with the mess. Or maybe she knew that Rory had done something and left. I couldn't help but believe the two of them really were brother and sister. The names weren't that common.

I found a website for her. There was only the one book. She had a lot of information on vampires and a list of her favorite vampire books, along with listing her own book on the page as "now available." Good for her, I thought. Perhaps Suzanne could look at the site and get ideas for marketing Olive's books, although given how well they were already selling, perhaps she'd already done that.

There was a single photo of Nancy on the 'about the author' page. It was small and hard to see. She looked like she was older than many of the people at the vampire conference. I would put her in her forties, which was about the age I had put the woman who had been looking for her earlier.

If she were really Rory's sister, he was around her same

age. Logan wasn't that much younger. I bit my lip trying to put these pieces together. Even if I managed to fit something together about the conference, there was Dale. I had no idea how he fit into this. No one had mentioned that Dale was into vampires.

I stood up suddenly as I had an aha moment and marched out to the desk. Mark had arrived and was already logging in. Suzanne was tucking away some paperwork.

"Okay, weird question. Do either of you know if Dale was into vampires? I mean, Rory is here for that conference so..." I trailed off.

"Not that I know of," Mark said. "Not that I knew him well."

"Me either," Suzanne said. "It's the sort of thing he might've been interested in, kind of counter culture and all, but I don't know for certain."

Well, there went that idea.

Sighing I started back towards my office. However, when I turned, I noticed Detective Granger and Detective Penn arriving at the hotel. The two of them together never boded well for me.

Chapter Twenty-Eight

Time seemed to slow down. Granger wasn't looking at me, exactly, which was fortunate. She seemed more zeroed in on Mark, which I didn't like. Suzanne seemed to notice it as well. The music from the bar changed, a low pop music tune that was made for slow dancing. It would have worked for a movie if the two of them were dating, though I doubted Granger dated anyone.

I had a moment to realize that Lyle called her by a nickname and wondered, but then shrugged it off. Lyle was quite a bit older than Granger. And he'd never said, although perhaps he wouldn't. I reminded myself not to be jealous as I watched the two detectives cross the white tile floor.

A couple of older people were there and one of them looked at the two and frowned, perhaps recognizing from the looks on their faces and the way they were dressed that we had police coming into the hotel. Again. Hopefully no one else was thinking *again* but me and my employees.

"Detectives," I said taking charge, "how can we help you?"

Granger glared at me. "I need to talk to Mark Harding."

"What about?" Mark asked.

"I have down here that you were at the Springs Bar and Grill the night Dale Benton was murdered," Granger said.

"I was."

"I also have down that you were seen talking to a man by the name of Rory Ingles that we're searching for."

Mark frowned. "I don't recall talking to anyone I didn't know. Not for any length of time."

Granger stood still and stared up at him.

Mark moved slightly as if he were uncomfortable, but Granger was good at making people sweat. I should know. She'd done it to me more than once.

"The bartender said that you talked to a man next to you, who matched the description of the missing Rory Ingles, for a good ten minutes while the bartender mixed drinks. Ingles then left the bar after chatting with you. I'd like to know what the conversation was about."

Mark continued frowning and then his expression changed. "There was a guy asking me about where to get groceries around here. He said he was at a hotel but didn't want to overspend on food. I figured it was our hotel and I explained where the grocery store was. I told him it was around the corner from the bookstore."

Granger waited. "Anything else you'd like to share?"

Mark thought about it. "I can't think of anything. The guy finished his drink and then left. I didn't get a name or anything."

"And you'd not seen him before, even though he was staying here. You said you figured that out from your conversation. But you didn't get a name?" Granger acted like that was akin to murder.

"I didn't," Mark said. "He looked sort of familiar, but I

see so many people. We're supposed to be friendly and all and I try to be, but names aren't really my thing."

Mark was far better at names than I was, but I didn't point that out. Instead, I just listened. Maybe I'd learn something.

"Are you sure he went to the grocery store?" Granger asked.

Mark shrugged. "I was at the bar for a few more drinks. I met up with a friend of mine and we chatted and had dinner. I didn't follow the man."

Granger closed her notebook.

I wondered if Dale had planned to meet Rory at the grocery store and for some reason Rory didn't want to admit that. The two seemed to be doing something rather under the radar, or so it seemed.

"Right now, Mr. Ingles joins Mr. Benton as a victim of whatever is going on here. And it seems to be focused around this hotel," Granger said, glaring at the three of us.

"Lyle said they were searching for Mr. Ingles," I replied. "He called because we'd been searching for Logan Fulton and I guess that's who reported the missing person."

"And it seems you've lost Mr. Fulton gain," Granger said. "The office had another call about him being missing. You'd think you could keep better track of your guests."

I bit back the fact that I wasn't their mother, again. What was it with people expecting me to know where everyone was at all times? I couldn't have done that in a bed and breakfast much less a hotel with as many rooms as we had.

"Well, as I've said before, we're a hotel. People come and go. They pay us for a room with a bathroom and a bed. We make sure it's clean and as safe as possible. We don't go around telling people what they can and can't do," I said, trying to smile. Considering how much it hurt, I was probably grimacing.

"What happened to Rory Ingles?" Suzanne asked. It should have been the first question on my mind, but Detective Granger had made me so angry.

"He's been found dead. Possibly exposure. We need to talk to Mr. Fulton some more," Granger said, keeping an eye on Suzanne. Penn stared at all three of us.

"I suppose you'll want to see his room," I said quietly, tapping on the keyboard to see what room Ingles was in.

"You don't need a warrant?" Granger asked.

"If he's dead, there's no expectation of privacy," I said. "And it sounds like he was someone known to the people at the conference, so you'll probably want to have someone questioning them downstairs. Many are just going to be getting to bed this time of day and will be up later in the afternoon."

"Why?" Granger asked.

"It's the Vampire Love Conference," I said.

Penn grimaced, though I knew he'd heard the name before. As if agreeing with my thought, he nodded.

Granger stared. It wasn't unlike Penn's original reaction.

"This just gets better and better," she said.

As if on cue, Lily hurried up to the desk and stood far too close to Detective Granger.

"Are you here to arrest her?" she demanded.

It surprised me that she knew Granger and Penn were police as both were in dark jeans and blazers. Penn did have a badge on his belt but that was all. Granger's wasn't even visible, though perhaps Lily had enough run ins with the law that she could spot them.

"And why should we do that?" Detective Granger

asked. It was done in a dry tone that held more humor than I would have expected from her, particularly if given the option of arresting me.

"She's using the name of my beloved cousin, Olive Hughes, for her own gain. She's gotten some attorney to make up some legal gobble-de-gook to keep my attorney from suing her for the royalties. She's even gotten someone to dress up like my cousin and say horrid things about me and my family!"

Granger looked from Lily to me. The look was definitely not friendly nor humorous.

"I'm not sure there's anything illegal about what you're talking about," Penn said. "And is probably best resolved through civil action, which your attorney can advise you on."

"Are you going to let us into the room or is someone else?" Granger asked, completely ignoring Lily.

"I can do it," I said, getting my pass card.

Lily, for her part glared at everyone involved.

"You haven't heard the last of me," she snapped before heading back to the café.

I was sure I hadn't, unfortunately.

Chapter Twenty-Nine

I led the detectives up to Rory's room. Letting people into rooms was getting to be a habit. At least this time, there shouldn't have been anyone inside. The hallway was quiet. I heard the television in a couple of rooms as we walked by them. Our feet made little noise on the carpet and Penn and Granger didn't speak to each other. Whether that was out of consideration for our guests who might be still trying to sleep or because they had nothing they wanted to say in front of me, was impossible to determine.

I knocked on Rory's door before using my key. It seemed the polite thing to do.

I frowned upon hearing someone moving around inside. A woman opened the door.

"Can I help you?" she asked.

"We're here about Rory Ingles," Detective Granger said. "Are you his wife?"

"Rory's not married," she said. "I'm Gail."

"Partner, girlfriend?" Granger pressed.

"What's this about?" she asked.

"If you'll tell us how you know Mr. Ingles, we'll be more forthcoming," Granger said. She pulled out her badge.

If the woman at the door was impressed, she didn't show it. Her straight dark hair was combed neatly and she had on blue jeans and a light plum colored sweater. It was the sort of outfit I could have pictured Olive wearing if Olive ever changed clothing. It just needed her pearls.

"I'd rather not," she said starting to close the door. Granger shouldered me out of the way and stuck her foot in the door.

"That's not an option," Granger said. "Rory Ingles was found dead in the park. We need to talk to the people who knew him. We need to know who you are and why you're in his room."

"I'm the one paying for the room," the woman said. "We're not together. More like friends with occasional benefits. Rory needed to be here and he wanted to save money so it made sense to share."

Personally, even if I were only friends with someone, I couldn't help thinking I'd be more upset to find out they were dead. This woman's attitude was incredibly cold. Or maybe it was shock. I probably shouldn't judge. I also found it interesting that although she was paying, the room was in Rory's name. Perhaps it had to do with the convention. It was something to look into later.

"We'll need to enter," Granger said.

"What if I don't give permission?" the woman said.

Granger pushed her aside, though I wasn't quite sure how legal that was. Penn moved in behind her. The woman glared at them and then shut the door in my face.

Sighing, I turned to go back downstairs.

"That was rude," Olive said appearing in the hallway

beside me. She'd spoken so quickly, I'd barely had time to get cool.

"It was. And strange. She didn't seem at all upset." I glanced back at the room as we walked along the hallway. I didn't need Detective Granger coming out and seeing Olive, not that most people realized she was a ghost. It seemed as if even Olive's family didn't quite recognize her now.

"Were they long time lovers? Perhaps they had a spat," Olive suggested.

"She said friends with benefits. Or rather occasional benefits, and it sounded like it was heavy on the occasional."

"What sort of benefits? Like hotel benefits?" Olive asked.

I wiped the smile off my face as I tried to decide how to explain that term to Olive. Given how savvy she was about certain modern things, I was a little surprised that she hadn't come across the term before.

As I gave her a general idea, Olive's face went slightly pink and she looked away.

"Oh dear. That is a new thought," she said. "But given that, I'd have thought she'd be more upset. Unless the benefits were not to her liking and then maybe she's the one who murdered him."

"And Logan Fulton is missing again," I said. "Also, your cousin Lily..."

"Lilianne," Olive corrected. "I don't care what she wants to be called. She's not earned my respect, so she can be called by her full name."

"Lilianne," I corrected, "came up to Detectives Granger and Penn and told them I ought to be arrested."

Olive rolled her eyes and dropped her head back. "Not

that I should be surprised. Lilianne was always like a dog with a bone once she got an idea in her head. And believe me, some of her ideas were outlandish."

"I just wish she wasn't so focused on me and the signature. It's like she knew I would be signing books at the store or something."

"If you hadn't been there, she probably would have berated Clay for carrying the books. That may have been why she went in to begin with. It's not like she's a book lover, or at least she wasn't when I was alive," Olive said. "She was too busy catering to her husband and telling other people what to do."

"Maybe her husband died or something and that's why she's so angry."

"Lilianne doesn't need a reason to be angry. And if her husband knew what was good for him, he'd have left her already."

I got into the elevator and Olive joined me.

"It's a lot, though," I said. "I mean with the murder—and, I guess, now, murders—the missing conference person, the annoying conference guests who seem to think the hotel should be taking care of everything, and her."

"You poor dear," Olive said, looking at me. It reminded me that Olive could be a caring person, even a caring boss when she wanted to be. "I forget how you can have so much on your plate sometimes. Perhaps go down to the spa and have a massage or get your hair done."

I gave her a tight smile and nodded. The elevator doors opened and I got out. Olive remained behind and I knew that when the doors closed and she was safely out of sight, she'd pop out and probably go hang around in Rory's room to see if she could see anything interesting. It was too bad

she couldn't hear. Not that it would stop her from material-
izing in a closet if the door was closed.

I could only hope that the woman in the room had the
good sense to keep that closet door closed so Olive could
listen in. Too bad I hadn't thought to suggest that to her.

Chapter Thirty

I crossed the white tiled floor to the reception desk and went in behind it. Suzanne and Mark were working away. Mark sent something to print and headed into the other room. I smelled the early morning smells of coffee and the slightly burned scent from the gas fireplace. It always happened shortly after it was lit.

"Did they find anything?" Suzanne asked me.

"Well, there was a woman in his room and she didn't seem at all happy to see the detectives. She claims they're friends with occasional benefits, but she didn't seem at all that upset when told that Rory was dead."

"Aren't friends with benefits always occasional?" Suzanne asked. "It's kind of the point."

"I wouldn't know," I said. I had no desire for that type of relationship. Things could get too messy too quickly. I'd actually have to advocate for myself and probably guard my space. Naturally, Lyle's face was the one that popped up in my mind and I pushed that thought away. I wasn't some lovesick teenager or lovesick anything.

"It's weird that she wouldn't look upset."

"I got the impression that she wasn't all that happy. Even Olive suggested that perhaps things weren't exactly benefiting the woman in the room," I explained.

"I'm surprised Olive knows that particular phrase."

"I got to explain it to her."

Suzanne laughed. While she is always polite and quite cheerful, I'd rarely heard her give a true guffaw. It was quite refreshing to hear. In fact, she ended up bent over the keyboard, her head down giggling.

Wiping her eyes as she straightened up, she spoke. "I'm sorry. The idea…"

"Yes, it wasn't the best moment in my life. I think Olive was a little sorry she'd asked."

"I can only imagine." Suzanne looked back at her keyboard.

I headed back into my office. I felt badly that another person was dead but I'd not had to discover the body and I'd not met the man. I mean, he was in my hotel, but I'd managed to never see him. Not that unusual as I manage the place and don't always work the front desk.

He had had an altercation with Logan earlier. Logan had been out hiking with him. It wasn't hard to put two and two together. I wondered if Logan's disappearances had anything to do with Rory's death. Considering Rory had been in town when Dale died, I wondered if Logan was on a murder spree or something.

Or maybe Rory was always the intended target and Dale got in the way.

I leaned my chin on my fist as I sat at my desk, thinking. I probably looked like a statue. I was trying to put every-thing together. I wondered what Nancy thought of her brother, assuming he was her brother. She'd left early. Perhaps she knew something was going on and didn't want to get involved. Smart on her part even if she didn't get a full refund on her booking. In fact, there wouldn't have been any refund as she'd booked through the conference site. Still, I needed to double check.

Logging on to the reservation system I looked at her booking. It was indeed through the Vampire Love Conference code. And she'd booked for several days. We had her credit card on file, but the room had been prepaid by Logan Fulton. Surprisingly, it appeared to be his personal account and not an account for the conference.

I called Susie.

"More complaints?" she asked without a greeting.

"Nothing for you, but be sure to give them our never again speech," I said. "What I wanted to know was that I saw the charges for one of the speakers who arrived and then left. It looked like the room had been prepaid. It was prepaid to a card issued in Logan's name rather than the name of the company."

Susie was silent for a few minutes, but I heard her tapping on the keyboard.

"There are four rooms charged to his personal account, although the conference card paid for the hospitality services. And he used the conference card for the deposits on the conference rooms as well."

"Interesting. Did he get a larger discount?" I asked.

"His room got comped along with a slight discount on food when the numbers went over a certain amount. He managed it, just. And right on the deadline, too. But the other rooms weren't."

"Who were the other people?" I asked.

"Nancy Ingles, Rory Ingles—if they're married it's weird they didn't have a single room—and Jimmy Caldwell."

Jimmy's name hadn't come up before. I'd have to look him up. I wondered who he was and what he was doing.

"Thanks for your help. I suppose I could have found that out on my own, but you made it easier," I said. I had access to Susie's files but the conference organizing system wasn't one I used as often and frequently had to backtrack on what I knew.

With a new name, I went back to my computer and started a search for Jimmy Caldwell. Unsurprisingly, his name was too common to be of any help. However, we'd gotten a driver's license when Caldwell checked in so I was able to narrow the search. He was from South Carolina, so he hadn't come far.

I found two profiles for people with his name from South Carolina on social media. One had a lot of nature stuff and pictures of trucks. The other was more locked down, but someone had posted some vampire memes to his account. Too bad I couldn't check him out further.

Doing a more general search, I did find a professional profile for someone who worked in engineering. Unfortunately, I don't know enough about the profession to figure out exactly what he did or didn't do. Caldwell appeared to be employed.

It surprised me to see that there were so many adults, who should have been mature, who were into vampires and spent money to go to conferences like Vampire Love. I would have expected it more of younger adults. Of course, if I were to go to a mystery conference, perhaps I'd find more younger adults there, too.

I decided to search Logan Fulton and Jimmy Caldwell together. Nothing came up. Then I had the idea to put in Rory Ingles and Dale Benton. After all, Rory supposedly went into town to see him, which was why the detectives had zeroed in on him.

Again, the search turned up nothing.

Sighing, I stretched and then went back to my spreadsheets and my list of calls I had to make and emails to follow up on. While I was distracted, I got some work done before lunch rolled around. No one had bothered me and no one called upon me to demand I perform some sort of miraculous thing to find a guest or solve a crime, though I wouldn't have minded doing the latter.

As I was about to leave, my phone rang. Lyle.

"Is everything all right?" I asked when I answered.

"I'm good. I just wanted you to know that the person we were searching for, Rory Ingles, was found. It wasn't a good ending."

"I heard. Detectives Granger and Penn were already here questioning some people," I said.

"Figured," Lyle said. "While it could have been an accident, it's equally possible that he was killed. Only the coroner will be able to tell us more."

"I heard Logan was taken to the hospital and then returned here. He's missing from the hotel again. I've had people asking for him," I said.

"He wasn't out at the trailhead," Lyle said. "I know he talked about wanting to find someone in town. Maybe he went there."

"Did you have a name?" I asked. Maybe Logan was also looking for Dale. Maybe Rory had killed Dale to keep him from talking to Logan.

"I think it was a woman, but I can't recall," Lyle said. "Not someone I know, so not on the force or someone connected to them."

He chuckled a little at his lack of variety in friends. I

was probably the only person he knew who wasn't in law enforcement or with the park service or connected to one of those professions in some way.

"Too bad. Might give me something to tell the people asking about him."

Lyle agreed. We talked a bit more before hanging up.

I pondered the conversation. Maybe I'd head into town and have a sandwich at Gloria's Deli. I didn't go there often, finding them slightly overpriced, considering I could eat at home or even on site with a discount for less, but her sandwiches were good. She used artisan breads and overstuffed them with meats and cheeses. My mouth watered just thinking about it.

Gloria also liked to talk about what was happening. I didn't go in often enough to be a confidant, but chances were someone else in there would be.

It was definitely time to head into town for lunch.

Chapter Thirty-One

After making sure that Suzanne and Mark were set for the lunch period, I took off for town. I'd been going back and forth to town more often than usual so I was going to have to stop for gas. Just another thing to add my list of things that weren't getting done. Of course, at least getting gas for my car was actually my responsibility and not something someone else was telling me I ought to do.

There was some traffic heading that way, but I still made good time. The clouds had darkened and by the time I got into Glade Springs, it was raining, though not very hard. When I parked, close to the deli, I was annoyed that I couldn't find an umbrella in my car. Instead, I had to hurry, holding my jacket closed, trotting into the building so I didn't get too wet.

The bell over the door rang as I stepped inside. I hadn't gotten so wet that I dripped on the black and white retro style tile floor. The glass door barely closed behind me. I noted the ten tables in a neat row along the window had plenty of patrons. Only two were still available, though a couple was getting ready to leave from one of them.

The small round chairs with a black back and white seat were being pushed neatly in, making only the slightest scraping sound. The cash register was in the far corner allowing the line to snake through the shop, while those waiting could look in and see the variety of deli meats, cheeses, and salads available for the day.

A young man was taking orders, but Gloria was working behind the counter making sandwiches faster than most people her age could move. She appeared to have a few years on me. The person ordering stepped to the side and the next person stepped up. I followed the woman in front of me.

"Don't know what the world is coming to. That poor man out in the woods," the man at the front said to Gloria as she whipped up a sandwich, probably his. She slathered the bread with mayonnaise and then added mustard with a practiced hand. I watched as she added what appeared to be a half pound of thin sliced ham and then several pieces of cheese.

The special that day was ham and jack cheese, but I preferred her turkey and Swiss. It really wasn't my day.

"He wasn't from around here, you know," Gloria said. "Not like Dale, which was bad enough, though Lord knows the boy had it coming a thousand ways to Sunday."

Her hands never stopped moving and she barely looked up as she spoke.

"A little surprised to hear about Dale. Not a nice guy, but not the sort anyone would murder," the guy said. "And in the old dojo? Just odd."

"Heard the owner caught him stealing," Gloria went on.

The line moved up one and the person who had

ordered went to stand next to the man. Gloria wrapped his sandwich carefully but just as quickly as she'd piled it with meats and cheeses.

"Yeah, but can't see Brett doing that. I took classes there." The speaker held the bag that had his sandwich but he was making no move to go.

"Heard there was bad blood, though," the woman who stood next to him said.

"Don't know the guy. He was into healthy eating and didn't come in here much," Gloria said. She kept on moving and while her hands flew over the sandwich fixings and she didn't look up, it was clear she knew her subject and probably better than she wanted to admit.

"Come on, Gloria, everyone knows you know everyone," the man said. He chuckled.

"I knew him from the town associations," Gloria said. "Seemed like a decent guy and all. And yeah, it would surprise me if the police are right on this, but it had to be someone."

"Clay had just as much reason if you're going that way," the woman said. "And you know he's frustrated with the bookstore and how it's doing. The online presence keeps them afloat and I know part of him wants to close up shop and just do the online store but Bill wouldn't hear of it."

"Or someone else would have to put up with Bill," the man said.

"I miss Bill," Gloria said. "He used to come in for lunch all the time. I had a special just for him."

"Clay would have to keep the books somewhere," the man said.

"I think a storage unit would be cheaper," the woman said. "And then he could rent out his space. Bill owned that building, you know."

"The town's not a great place for commercial rentals," Gloria said. "We don't have the population. There'd be three or four different places in that spot in a year."

"And Clay would spend on doing buildouts."

The three of them commiserated.

"Anyone meet the other guy who died?" the next person in line asked as he walked over. He gave a wave to the original man who'd been talking to Gloria. This guy was younger and broader than the first man.

"Nah. He was just visiting. I think he was at some conference out at the Neary-Ten."

"Some weird conference," Gloria said. "Vampires and stuff. I mean, I liked some of those series and all and that movie Twilight or whatever, but I can't imagine wanting to go to a conference about them."

"The food out there is high if you're paying on your own. Love my Friday nights for pizza but can't imagine having to put out for their dining venues for four or five days," the guy said.

It was my turn at the register so I missed the next part of the conversation, which wasn't a horrible thing. I didn't want to get drawn into a discussion on prices. I thought they were fair. The young man at the register was blonde and blue eyed and didn't look like he'd started shaving. I was surprised that someone so young would be behind the counter during the day while school was in session.

I ordered my sandwich and went to stand with the others. More tables were available and someone had come from the back to wipe down several. I saw the same girl come out with more sliced bread for sandwiches. Gloria didn't pause and her hands kept moving. The woman who had come up to talk left with her bag of food but the two men were still there talking. The woman in front of me was seated at a table.

"I swear that Dale was after his ex again," the other man said, keeping his voice low.

"Teena?" Gloria asked.

I filed that away. There was a Teena in my class. I thought that I had heard she was Dale's ex as well, though it had been quite some time.

"You know they're on again, off again. Don't know why she puts up with it. Last time, she ended up in the hospital, poor thing," the man said. "My cousin is an EMT, you know."

"She comes in here regular," Gloria said. "Teena's such a little thing. I can't imagine she'd be able to take out Dale. Why he kept hitting her when they were together, I don't know. Might have been the first time she ended up in the hospital, but not the first time she got herself hit."

Gloria glanced up at the computer screen telling her what sandwiches to make and then she was back at it, her hands flying over the bread as if they knew the recipes every bit as well as her mind. Given how long she'd been in business, perhaps they did.

"She's got some relatives out of town. Heard her best friend from school was supposed to be in town but she didn't show," the man said.

"Teena didn't go to high school here, though. Her folks moved when she was in her twenties and then she moved here. She'd have been better off staying down in the big city."

I wasn't certain which big city Gloria was referring to. To someone from Glade Springs, Hickory might be a big city, though I suspect she meant Winston-Salem although

Raleigh-Durham wasn't out of the question either. North Carolina liked to combine city names it seemed.

But it would make sense then, if someone she knew from school had been here. I thought about Nancy. She was around Teena's age. Maybe she set her brother up to murder Dale. Of course, then I had to wonder why Rory had gotten himself killed. It didn't really make sense to me, so I had something wrong.

When my sandwich was up, I reluctantly took it, not wanting to miss more conversation but also not wanting to hang around and perhaps have people wonder who I was and why I was listening in. And from what the man standing there talking to Gloria had said, he was not a huge fan of the Neary-Ten, so I wanted to avoid answering questions.

Seated, I ate my sandwich wondering what my next move should be. The rain splashed down outside, coming down hard enough to make the little deli sound like the inside of a drum being played by a five year old.

It didn't put me off the lunch. The sandwich was far better than anything I made for myself and different from the food we served at the hotel. By the time I had finished eating, the talkative man had left and Gloria was talking to someone else.

"Al and Ed were in the bar the other day," the woman was saying as I passed by to put my garbage in the trash.

I slowed as I walked by, figuring she was talking about Alice Granger and Edward Penn, the detectives.

"Heard Mark Harding was there talking to the guy who got himself killed," Gloria said. "Course Mark's the only decent one of the clan. Works hard up at the hotel. Really turned his life around, though why he helps out some of the rest of the family, I'll never know."

"Yeah, Mark wouldn't hurt a fly. Remember when he got beat up by Jones Barlow?" the woman said.

Gloria laughed. "His daddy was so mad at him for not fighting back. That man ain't the least bit proud of that boy not heading to jail and getting on the right side of life. Ought to be, you know?"

I continued on my way, tossing my garbage, glad to hear that my trust in Mark was not misplaced. For all that we had worked together for years, I didn't know a lot about Mark's past. I knew, generally, that he came from a family that was often on the wrong side of the law, but that was about it.

The rain had let up a bit when I left the deli. I hurried down to my car, which was parked about halfway to the bookstore. I decided to stop in at the Cornered Reader just to see if Clay or Bill knew anything more.

Chapter Thirty-Two

It started to sprinkle again before I got to the bookstore, but I wasn't too wet when I ducked inside. Soft music greeted me along with the squeak of the floorboards. A couple of people were talking to Clay up at the desk. I recognized one of them as Teena Anderson, the woman from my dojo, who had supposedly dated Dale at one point.

Clay nodded at me and then gestured behind him to the books. Teena squealed like a teenager, though she isn't much younger than I am, and hurried over to me, arms out.

"I'm so thrilled that you wrote a book! I know an author!" she said. Her voice had the low scratchy quality of a long-time smoker, though I didn't smell cigarettes on her. Perhaps the martial arts was just one part of her goals to get healthier and she'd stopped smoking as well.

"Thanks," I said, smiling. I tried to decide if I ought to tell her Olive actually wrote it and I just signed things.

Clay chuckled a little. Suzanne had probably told him the truth but no one was going to out Olive to strangers which was both a good and bad thing for me. Good in that I appreciated their loyalty and I didn't have to explain how I got roped into being the face of her books, and bad in that people thought I wrote books, which I most certainly do not.

Teena gushed a bit more. Her hair, that day, was white blonde. Other times it was purple. She had it cut very short, almost shaved on one side. Her narrow face was lined and her skin was dry and crinkly, as if she were far older than she was.

"I can't wait to talk more when Brett gets the dojo up and running again," Teena said. She clapped her hands. "Of course, I'm hoping for a little one-on-one with *him* before then, if you know what I mean!"

She laughed at the innuendo and slipped out with her friend, an equally blonde woman dressed in too tight jeans and a t-shirt that showed off the curve of breasts that hung a bit too far down her chest to be particularly sexy looking. Not that mine were any perkier, but I'd discovered bras that actually held them up.

"Despite the books having to be behind the counter, I've nearly sold out," Clay said happily. "Of course, in some ways, it's been a good conversation starter because people ask why they're all back there and I explain what happened. I think some people purchased just because they don't like the idea of someone trying to bully a local author."

"Interesting," I said. It seemed that although by Glade Springs standards I was an outsider, at least I was less of an outsider than someone like Lily, who was only visiting.

"If they're buying and you and Suzanne are getting the royalties, it's all good to me. At least I hope it doesn't help Olive's relative, does it?"

I told him about the call from the attorney.

"Sounds like they don't think she really has a case,

which is good." Clay nodded to himself. "Can I help you find anything?"

"Just kind of browsing and getting out of the rain. Did you hear about the guest who was found dead in the woods?" I asked, hoping to hear something from Clay.

"Everyone's heard. It's horrible. First Dale and then him. I heard they knew each other. Kind of makes you wonder if they were in on something together."

"I can't imagine what. Rory was just visiting."

"Doesn't meant they weren't in regular contact. The internet keeps people connected even if they don't live nearby. I think Dale and Rory go way back."

"I heard something about that at Gloria's."

"Ah the gossip shop!" Clay laughed. He picked up a pile of books and placed it on a cart to take back to shelf.

"I ought to let you get to work." I moved over to the tables across from the counter and started to browse those books. I didn't see anything that struck my fancy so I wandered over to Bill and settled in the chair.

"Rainy day," he said. "I used to love rain, but it drove the customers away because no one wants to be out in it."

I agreed with him.

"Heard about that Rory," Bill said changing the subject. "He knew Dale?"

"That's what I hear," I said.

"I was thinking about it. I was up in the window the other night, but I'm not sure it's the night Dale died. But there were trucks across the way. Saw a bunch of guys go in. Then I saw a woman go in. She came out and drove the truck away after another car pulled in."

My heart thudded. If he was remembering correctly, he'd seen the killer.

"You might have seen the killer," I said. "Did you get a good look at her?"

"My eyes aren't any better as a ghost than they were in life," he said sadly. "I knew it was a woman from the way she walked. Can't quite put my finger on how that's different, but it is."

"Anything else?"

"She was short. Not much taller than Detective Granger, if I recall, although you can always tell her from the way she marches around like she's a big dog or something." Bill chuckled at the image.

I bit back a laugh at the thought that he was comparing Detective Granger to a little dog posing as a big dog. I doubt she'd take kindly to being compared to a chihuahua. I didn't particularly like her, but I wasn't sure that was a fair comparison.

Teena was short but not that short. Of course, Bill had been further away and maybe he wasn't good at judging the distances. Of course, Teena also walked with a definite swing to her hips, something that would have been easy enough to see. I mentally crossed her off the list. That left me with the mysterious Nancy but I couldn't figure out why she'd have murdered Dale. We really knew nothing about her.

"Do the detectives know about you?" I asked Bill.

He shrugged. "I sit here. They come in. They see me but don't really interact. I assume they know I used to run the place. Why?"

"Just wondering if they could come in an ask you questions," I said.

"The problem is, I can't always remember things clearly," Bill said. "I sit here so much or else look out the side window upstairs and everything runs together. I might have a clear image of things and remember what was going on, but I can't guarantee I'd recall something exactly when asked, not unless someone fed me what I'd said before."

I felt badly for him and hoped that Olive wouldn't become like that. Of course, things changed around the hotel all the time. And Olive seemed more likely to forget things from earlier in her life.

"Still, maybe tell Clay and have him talk to the police," I said. "If it came up in court, maybe he could say he was at the window."

Bill nodded, but I wasn't sure he was agreeing with me or just being thoughtful. It was hard to say.

I thanked him for his time and wandered out of the bookstore. The rain was coming down again and I had to run to my car. I slipped inside and shivered. I started the car and then got out my phone to see what I could find out about Nancy Ingles. It suddenly seemed important to know more about her. She was definitely a key to what was happening.

Chapter Thirty-Three

I stopped around the corner for gas, despite being soaked through. I was the only one doing so, as most people had the sense to be inside. I had no doubt there would be plenty of people driving along the highway, but in town, anyone who could stay inside was doing so.

Shivering a bit, I avoided stepping in any puddles lest they contain traces of gasoline and I'd have the fumes following me home. It was a smell that I disliked and had no desire to carry it into my car.

The gas station was on the other side of the grocery store. At one time, I'd heard it was a small family-owned place, but now it was one of the chains that had popped up all over the place, and despite being next door to a grocery store, it had one of the convenience stores that so many had now. The prices there were much higher, though, and I often wondered how it was financially sound to have the building.

Glade Springs was a couple of miles off the highway but the exit had a gas station and a Burger King right there, so travelers had little reason to come all the way into town for gas. I had heard that the station by the grocery store offered very nice homemade breakfast biscuits and pancakes in the morning, though I'd not come into town to try them.

Lyle told me that he sometimes enjoyed them.

Finishing my task with a shiver, wishing I could smell bacon and sausage rather than gasoline fumes, I slipped back into my car. I noticed Brett's car driving down the street towards the dojo. I waved, but he didn't see me.

Biting my lip, I pulled out onto the street. When Brett's car made the turn into the dojo and just sat there, I decided that perhaps he needed a friend and I followed him into the place.

Noticing another car, he got out and hurried over to the building's overhang, which sheltered him from the rain. I followed.

"Is everything okay?" I asked. "I hope that you'll still be able to make the updates."

"It's going," Brett said. "I think the police are finally not stuck on me as the culprit. Dale was a jerk, but I wouldn't murder him for his jokes. Sad as it is for the other guy killed in the woods, the police seem to think they're linked and that lets me out."

"Good to hear," I said. "I was worried about the rumors floating around. I can't see you hurting anyone—I mean not like that..."

That was not quite what I meant to say.

"I've heard Teena Anderson has ties to both men, but while she tries, she's not exactly my star pupil."

I nodded. Teena had been part of the jiu jitsu class longer than I had. She still struggled with most forms. Or, thinking about her commentary about wanting personal attention from Brett, maybe it was an act. Still, it was hard to see her overpowering someone like Dale.

"I have a hard time seeing her overpowering someone." I stood with my back to building looking out at the occasional passing car. No one stopped. A single white car turned into the grocery store parking lot, but no one got out, the driver probably waiting until the rain stopped. I wondered what Brett and I looked like standing under the front cover of a condemned building.

"I'm sorry you had to find him," Brett said. "The police told me. I knew that people had left things in the lockers and I cleared them before the workers went through. I have them in plastic bags and containers. Alyssa helped."

"Thanks. I should have called. Of course, then someone else would have found him." Or perhaps he would have just disappeared if the killer had been interrupted.

"The workers are upset. No one really enjoyed working with him, but still, no one wanted him dead. They just wanted him on someone else's team."

Brett stared straight ahead.

"Do you know anyone named Nancy Ingles?" I asked.

Brett paused, clearly thinking. "I've heard the name, but can't place where."

We stood in silence. I wondered if maybe the police had asked him about her, but didn't want to make him think that was where he heard it. If he'd met her elsewhere, I wanted to know. Maybe that would be the key to solving the mystery.

"We were in a tournament together, in Las Vegas. It's been years which is why I didn't directly recall. She's good."

"She was at the hotel that night but checked out around midnight. I was wondering if she was related to the man who died in the woods."

I also wondered if Nancy was short. I hadn't found any photos of her, though I had little information on her to work with. And she was old enough that she might not have used social media as regularly as some of the younger people did.

"Interesting," Brett said. "She'd be more likely to kill someone than Teena. Not that she was mean or anything, it's just that she was really good. She didn't just study jiu jitsu. I think as a child she'd started with tae kwon do and had a black belt in that. She said jiu jitsu was easier because she was short and carried her weight in her legs."

Nancy could easily have been the person Bill saw in the window. Things were coming together. I just didn't know why she'd murdered Dale or where she was just then.

The rain began to lessen.

"We ought to get going," Brett said.

"You came here for something," I said.

He sighed. "I just wanted to get a look at the place. They've released it and they're going to demo it tomorrow. The entire thing. While I started the process, I'm still a little sad. I put in a lot of work to get it looking like it is."

"How long were you here?"

"About six years. Bought the place after my third year when the previous owner decided to sell. I had an inspection and there wasn't any water damage then. I guess the pipe problems started after. Just my luck." Brett shook his head. "But at least insurance pays for some of this because of the damage. And I'm renting the old K-mart space for workouts starting next month."

I knew the building he meant. It hadn't been a K-mart for a couple of decades but everyone remembered it. It had been the largest store in town and the one place you could go and get stuff that you might not find in the grocery store. Now we had a couple of dollar stores and that was it. Both were smaller and didn't have the variety of K-mart.

When it was open, even I had shopped there. Of course,

I'd lived in the apartments not far from it when I'd started, considering I wasn't a manager. Bill had still run the bookstore and I'd stopped in more often on my days off, which actually was time off. I had a moment of nostalgia for times past.

I stepped off the porch and got in my car. Brett was still there, looking at the building, running his hands along the door. I wondered if he'd painted the red door himself. Then he shook his head and turned. When I drove out, he was getting in his car.

Returning to the hotel, I promised myself I'd find out who this Nancy Ingles really was. Hopefully, Detective Granger also knew that Nancy had martial arts background and was looking for her as well.

Chapter Thirty-Four

The drive wasn't bad. The sun even peeked through the gray clouds once and then quickly disappeared behind even darker clouds. It was nearly as dark as night when I pulled into the underground parking space that afternoon. I hurried out of my car and started to walk towards the door to the hotel.

Something moved in the garage and I froze, listening. The main door worked with our keycards. The restaurant managers had spaces down there as well. It wasn't impossible that a raccoon or squirrel had timed its entrance just right, but it was unlikely.

My car was the one closest to the door that would take me to the hallway to the main part of the building or else up the stairs to the restaurant. There were two other cars in the garage, a large black SUV, which I knew belonged to the head chef, and a smaller sedan in beige which I thought belonged to our evening restaurant manager.

The sound came again, a scurry but a large scurry, too heavy sounding for a squirrel and not even something I'd associate with a raccoon. I fumbled in my purse looking for my card so I could head into the hotel. My hands were shaking and I dropped my purse on the floor and had to scramble to pick everything up.

I heard footsteps moving around. I stood up, my car keys in hand. I considered jumping in my car and fleeing. I didn't want to be alone in the garage with someone. No one appeared and for a moment I wondered if it were one of our ghosts.

Then someone hit me from behind and I slammed down with barely time to protect my face. Still, the fall left me with a headache and I worried one of my eyes might bruise and blacken where one of my knuckles pressed into it when I fell. A foot kicked me in the side. I groaned only slightly, trying to figure out why someone would lie in wait for me in the garage.

I blacked out only to come to as my body was being dragged across the cement floor. My coat would be in filthy and possibly even ruined by the concrete and any oil that might have leaked onto the floor. Then my mind cleared enough to for me to be terrified that my coat was the least of my worries. Someone was dragging me away from my car and my purse.

Groaning I attempted to keep my eyes open but closed them again as some dust from the floor floated up and stung. My hands were pulled behind my back.

The garage had cameras by the main doors and by the door to the hotel. There weren't any inside the place because we'd decided that someone would see the person driving in or walking in and then going into the building so there wasn't a reason to have one looking at the cars. After all, it was a handful of staff with a door that required not just any keycard but a special manager level keycard.

We changed those out regularly. While no one looked

for people when they drove in, it would be easy enough to see someone running into the garage itself, if not by the person driving, then by security. And yet, someone had lain in wait down there.

If this was Nancy, it must have been where she was hiding. Maybe I'd interrupted whatever it was she was doing down there when I'd come in. I couldn't fathom why she'd attack me. She'd already killed two people. Fortunately, neither of them had been in my hotel.

When she stopped dragging me, I opened my eyes just a slit. I really didn't want her to know I was awake nor did I want dust in them. It wasn't as if I could wipe them if that happened. The woman in the garage was short, with gray hair that barely covered her ears. She wore jeans and a sweatshirt. Her sneakers left damp footprints on the concrete.

The dampness reminded me how cold it was and I was already feeling the temperature change from the floor. I kept my breathing even, wondering what she was doing. For the moment she was looking at the things I had dropped. Maybe she was looking for my key. It was a stupid way to get into the hotel. She could have walked in the front and no one would have noticed.

As I had time to focus, I noticed a small pile of items in a corner than I hadn't seen before. Perhaps she'd been staying in the garage, or camping there. I wondered how long she'd been down there.

I closed my eyes again, wondering why she was doing this. The whole thing was weird.

"Get down here," she said. I didn't hear anyone but figured she'd made a phone call.

Hopefully she wasn't using my phone to call someone I knew down to the garage. Of course, there was a camera at the door to the hotel and another at the entry to the garage.

She wasn't using the speaker so I couldn't hear the other side of the conversation.

"I don't care how you do it, just figure it out. I slipped in with a car and hid on the side. No one came down. There aren't any cameras inside. The ones here face towards the outside so they can see people going in and out. There's probably one into the basement of the restaurant but I don't see one in here and I've been looking."

More silence. She was right about the placement. If I survived this, we'd be adding more to the garage. Of course, the chances of someone else being hurt or attacked in the garage were almost non-existent.

"Well, I've got her here," the woman said. "She drove in just now. I knocked her out and haven't had a chance to ask her what she was doing in Rory's room or yours."

More silence.

"I don't think she found anything but I'll find that out."

A brief silence, not nearly long enough for me to think about what I might have seen out of place in either room.

"Then we take care of her...I said *we* because you're helping this time. I'm not doing all the work."

I listened as the woman who had to be Nancy paced around on the concrete. I smelled her before I saw her. She stank of body odor and something metallic with an underlying hint of rosemary that was probably more her natural smell.

Chill hands patted my cheek. I groaned a little but didn't open my eyes, hoping that was good enough acting for her. I didn't want her to think I was awake and aware. I needed to stall as long as possible in hopes that perhaps security would notice something or maybe one of the restaurant staff would forget something in their car, though I had little hope of either of those things.

My phone rang. It was all I could do to cover the start by moving my head side to side as if I were almost waking up.

Nancy didn't move to get it. She sat far too close to me, her breath warm on my face. She hadn't brushed her teeth that morning and the last thing she'd eaten had been spicy, though I wasn't sure what the spice was.

I didn't let myself react. With her so close, I couldn't even attempt to see if I could break out of whatever she'd tied my hands with. It felt like something with a knot rather than zip ties, which I wouldn't have been able to break. At least I had a chance, if only she'd stand and move further way.

The fact that my hands were tied made me wonder how long I'd been out. Eventually, Suzanne and Mark would notice I'd been gone longer than I should have been. It was even possible that whoever called my phone was one of them. I could only hope that my lack of answering would make them worry and that they'd check security.

The woman patted my face again.

"I know you're awake and just faking it. You did a decent job up until your phone rang. Too bad for you," Nancy said.

I kept my eyes closed, deciding if it was worth it to stay that way.

Nancy slapped my face again, this time harder.

I opened my eyes in shock.

"Yeah, I see you. Who are you?"

"Maggie Davenport," I said.

"And why were you in Logans's room? What were you looking for? What did they tell you?"

"Two other guests came to me looking for Logan. No one answered on the room phone and they'd knocked on the door but no one answered. They were worried something had happened to him. I went up to see if he were there."

"Who were these people?" Nancy seemed agitated now.

"I don't know. Just guests. There were two women who've been worried about finding Logan this whole conference. He seems to have been missing most of it, although I guess he turned up out in the woods at one point. But lots of speakers didn't show up and the conference attendees were angry."

"And why did they go to you to get into the rooms? Did they pay you? Tell you you could get money?"

"It's always best if the hotel manager does the entry to a room. I've even let police officers into a room when needed. Unless we know that say, the person is deceased and no one should be in the room, I typically do the room opening."

Nancy snorted.

I said nothing. I could have asked what was so funny. In my mind the fact that she was probably planning on killing me for nothing more than doing my job was probably the reason.

Nancy got up and paced around. She pulled out her phone and then set it back. She kicked mine under the car at one point, but she kept pacing.

I worked the knots on the ties on my hands. In the movies it always seems fairly easy. It might take a bit of work but eventually they do it, or if they're Jack Reacher, they just break them. I wasn't able to do either of those things, but not for lack of trying. In books, perhaps the main character would dislocate a thumb to get out of handcuffs and ties but I couldn't imagine doing that. My wrists hurt just from the rope or whatever was used to tie my hands.

From the feel of it, the hairy scratchiness, I was guessing some sort of twine, which would make sense if Nancy had planned on camping. When I was a child, my family camped a lot. As I grew older, I got tired of the discomfort of the forest floor and took a liking to my own bed and comfortable bathroom.

My sister still camped, although she wasn't that much younger than I was. Now, she took an inflatable mattress because her back didn't like sleeping on the hard ground any longer. When I suggested she spring for a hotel, she'd laughed at me as if I were making a joke. It just proves that we don't always have that much in common with our family.

Someone moved around outside, but they didn't come in. If Nancy had called someone, perhaps Logan, then maybe he couldn't figure out how to get into the garage. It's not like you could just walk or drive in without a special key card. At least they'd be on camera coming in. Given how they were moving around, security couldn't miss them. Maybe that would even catch security's interest and someone would come over and investigate.

My hopes rose a bit more than they had been as I had been sitting there wondering if I was going to survive. The person outside left again.

Nancy's phone rang.

"Yeah?"

"I can't let you in. You have to sneak in. Try through the restaurant, though wear a mask when you get down here because I'll bet there's a camera there. If there's not, we're lucky but I would assume there is."

She dropped the phone back into her pocket and kept

on pacing. She started mumbling to herself but I couldn't figure out what she was mumbling. If only Olive could get to the parking garage. She could see what was going on and let someone know.

The restaurant had its own ghost. I hadn't ever seen Smithers in the parking garage, though that didn't mean he didn't go there. It was part of the basement in the restaurant. We had storage in one portion and the garage in the rest. Smithers could go just about anywhere in the restaurant though he preferred the attic and sometimes the main floor.

"Come on Smithers. If you were ever going to be a help, now would be the time to do it," I muttered, hoping it wouldn't attract Nancy's attention. It didn't seem to. She was lost in her own thoughts.

"What were you worried I'd find?" I asked.

Nancy whirled, almost like she'd forgotten I was there.

"What do you mean?"

"You seemed worried that I'd find something in Rory's room or maybe Logan's. What was it?"

She glared at me and turned away as if my question was beneath her.

"We're just sitting here waiting. If you want someone to come in here, they have to come through the restaurant or they need a keycard. You can get out without one through the outer doors but not the one into the building. We wanted people parking here to be safe."

Nancy said nothing. She kept pacing and mumbling.

It was becoming annoying and a little scary. I worried that she was losing touch with reality, as if that would make her even more dangerous.

"Why did you kill Dale Benton?" I asked.

Nancy stopped. She didn't turn. I saw her shoulders raise and fall.

"Dale knew about Logan," she whispered. "And he told Rory. Logan was only doing it to help me. Rory certainly wouldn't. And Dale was going to tell Rory or maybe he did tell him."

I wanted to know what Logan had done for her but my phone rang again, distracting both of us, but especially Nancy.

"Someone is trying hard to get you," she said. "Who did you tell? You know more than what you're saying!"

I shook my head. "I'm the hotel manager. If someone needs something that my regular staff can't handle, they'll want to get a hold of me."

It was true enough but it was unlike Suzanne and Mark not to figure something out for themselves. For all I knew, Detective Granger was attempting to get a hold of me because she decided I knew something. She and Nancy had more in common than they knew. Of course, the worst thing Granger could do was put me in jail. I had a feeling Nancy might try and murder me.

"You could tell me what's going on," I said when the ringing stopped.

Nancy glared. "I won't tell you anything."

The door to the garage opened. My heart sank. I thought of the people in the kitchen who might have tried to stop a stranger hurrying through. Or perhaps they all cheered if he gave them a story. With Logan there, no one would come and rescue me.

I couldn't see who it was at first. Nancy was standing closer and she took a step backwards, towards the garage door rather than towards me. I couldn't imagine who would frighten her.

"Drop any weapons and put your hands on your head," a woman's voice said. The low growl that the words were said with told me it was Detective Granger. She was about the last person I expected to rescue me, but at the same time I was relieved.

"I think she's in this with Logan Fulton," I called out. "She thinks I saw something in either Logan or Rory's rooms when I went searching for Logan for another guest."

"We know," Granger said. "Logan confessed. We've been searching for him. We caught him after picking him up on the outside security camera. He was more than happy to share what was going on."

Nancy fell to her knees.

Detective Penn came over and undid the knots around my wrists with an ease that embarrassed me for not being able to get them off. He asked if I were injured. I looked down at my coat which was filthy and there were some places that the cloth had ripped.

"I'm okay, but I think my clothing has seen better days."

I had a bit of savings which I'd be dipping into to get a new coat. I couldn't go through the winter without one and this one was probably not salvageable, though I could go into town and see if the people at the laundry could do it. They did do mending for a hefty fee for people who needed it.

Penn helped me up, but he did ask me to stick around because they'd called the EMTs, not certain what shape I'd be in. I dusted myself off as well as I could. I did feel a little dizzy and didn't move far from a wall where I could be sure I could lean if necessary.

"What was it she thought I saw?" I asked.

"Nancy had cancer a couple of years ago. Used up her long-term disability and still couldn't work. She was finally fired from her job and lost her insurance. She was about to end up living in her car. She and her brother knew Logan, so he threw her some work speaking at the conference, but it wasn't enough. He wanted to impress her by helping more, so he embezzled funds from the conference. Though he did try to pay some of it back. He managed to keep the conference from being cancelled, but the payments for most speakers and even their travel arrangements were gone, so most didn't come," Granger said.

"My brother found out and was pissed off," Nancy said. "Not that we did it, but because we didn't cut him in. He was bitching to Dale and together they said they wanted their share of the money. I'd paid the rent on my apartment already and didn't have anything left. Logan had paid for my trip here. Heck, he was already covering the hotel costs for Rory and another speaker, one that he knew would make a stink if things weren't paid on time."

"Dale was being pushy and I got mad and hit him. I didn't realize he was half drunk already and went down hard. I kept kicking him, trying to wake him..."

"Or make sure he was dead," Granger interjected.

Nancy said nothing. "Then I ran."

"Rory stayed behind, hoping that Dale wasn't really dead, but when he couldn't find a pulse, he started wiping down finger prints and stuff," Granger said. "He had hoped Dale would take him back to the hotel so he grabbed the keys and planned on driving himself back. He didn't want anyone to see him at the dojo. You came in about the time he was getting ready to leave. He ducked down behind the reception desk."

"He tried to blackmail Logan then, figuring I wouldn't kill him. Logan got him out of the hotel so I could kill him in the woods. We didn't need another body turning up. Unfortunately, Logan got lost," Nancy shook her head as if Logan was an idiot. She was probably right.

"But what would I have seen?" I asked.

Granger picked up the story again.

"Rory had left Logan a note that said he wanted money. He knew about how much Nancy had gotten from the Logan's embezzlement and Rory wanted a portion of that. He outlined it in a note. We had the letter, but it wasn't signed. Logan could have been trying to blackmail Rory for all we knew." Granger watched as Penn made sure that the cuffs were on Nancy's hands.

I'd not even noticed the paperwork, nor I had I looked for anything. All of this was because Nancy was paranoid. And it had gotten her caught.

"Have you been staying down here all this time?" I asked.

"Since Rory died in the woods," Nancy said proudly. "Your security sucks."

I'd let Jake know her opinion and we'd get an extra garage camera. I'd make sure it was in the budget. I had no doubt Ari would make sure it was approved if it was a large expenditure, but given the way people had cameras everywhere, I doubted it would be.

The EMTs arrived and checked me out. They wanted to take me to the local clinic and I agreed, though first I wanted my purse and my phone.

"Was it you who kept calling me?" I asked Granger.

She shook her head.

I looked at the number. It had been the attorney's office. My stomach knotted as I wondered what new thing Lily had tried.

Chapter Thirty-Five

The EMTs didn't let me use my phone and because I was brought in by ambulance, I didn't get a chance to return the call. The nurses and doctors were very prompt about checking me over, further preventing me from calling the paralegal back. All of this worried me and stressed me, as if I didn't have enough to worry about after practically being murdered in the parking garage of the hotel.

Lyle arrived with Suzanne after that. He'd heard about the incident over the police radio and had hurried to the hotel, only to find that I wasn't there. Having heard what happened from him, Suzanne insisted upon riding along, though I had no doubt Olive wouldn't be happy about that. She'd be annoyed that she couldn't come. It was too bad there wasn't a way for her to leave the hotel.

"I'm fine," I told them as they hovered over the bed where I was resting. At least I hadn't been forced into a gown, though my coat had been taken off and I had my sleeves rolled up for the blood pressure cuff that measured blood pressure every few minutes.

"I had no idea," Suzanne said. "I called Jake when we left and he knew. I guess he's already looking into adding a camera in the garage."

"I was going to talk to him about that. Oh, and while I was there, the paralegal that I engaged kept calling me. There were three calls from her. I really want to find out what's going on."

Suzanne was kind enough to grab my phone for me. She and Lyle sat there and listened in while I called the direct number.

"Oh, I'm so glad I got you before the end of the day. Tomorrow, I'm having someone send some paperwork for you to sign. Morgan McDaniel sent over a file that shows that he's dropping the lawsuit and you need to sign a copy that you're aware of that. If you need to take out a restraining order against Lily or anything, that will be separate. Realize that Morgan's paperwork just says he is dropping the case and not that Lily is agreeing not to refile."

"Do you think she can?"

"Anyone can do anything. She still doesn't have cause," the paralegal said.

"Thanks for letting me know."

"I got a call from another attorney and I told her the same thing I told McDaniel. She quickly hung up. I have a feeling Lily is attorney shopping. This could drag on for a bit."

Sighing, I hung up and told Suzanne and Lyle what the paralegal had said.

"Too bad," Suzanne said. "I'm glad that you, well we, have an attorney who knows the law, though."

I nodded.

Lyle patted my hand.

"I had no idea that Logan was part of the plot to murder Rory."

"I'm not sure he knew that Nancy was killing people. I think maybe he was scared and was doing what she told him to. He seemed to break down and give an awful lot of detail to Detective Granger."

"What Granger didn't tell you is that they found him earlier. He was only outside of the garage because he was afraid of Nancy and wanted her to think he was still helping her. If Granger hadn't heard you talking through the door they were listening at, they were going to see if sending Logan in would get her to confess her part in things," Lyle said.

Well, at least I was useful for something.

A nurse bustled in bringing with her a fresh whiff of the lovely hospital scent that permeated everything. She checked my blood pressure and looked me over once more.

"Except for that bout of dizziness and some minor cuts that you'll need to keep an eye on, the doctor says you're good to go," the nurse said.

"Great," I started to get up.

"Just wait. We need to go through the check out procedures and have a doctor sign off. You can chat with your friends, but it could be a bit. We have a couple of other people here," she said before leaving us to my cubicle.

We all looked at each other and tried to make conversation.

"It's funny that after talking to Bill and then to Brett while I was in town, I was going to research Nancy Ingles," I told them. "She just found me before I did. I guess she's been hiding in the garage for a couple of days."

"That's what I heard," Lyle said. I really wanted to

know what his source was. I needed to know things like that.

"I can't figure out how she could hide there. Not all cars are there at all times," Suzanne said.

"But my car is almost always there," I said. "And even when I go out, it's usually day time so there are two other cars down there she could hide behind. It's not like anyone ever looks to see if someone else is there. The garage is pretty secure."

"I suppose," Suzanne said.

"Does Olive know?" I asked.

"Oh yeah," Suzanne said. Lyle nodded along.

"She listened in while I told Suzanne what had happened. She's mad that she missed the detectives working with Logan down in the security office. They wired him up there," Lyle said.

"She said she could have used that in her next book," Suzanne smiled.

I nodded, knowing I was going to have a lot of explaining to do when I returned to the hotel. Just as well that the doctor had other patients to attend it. It would give me some time to relax a bit and get myself together before sharing everything with Olive.

Chapter Thirty-Six

Olive didn't exactly give me much time to decompress and figure out what I wanted to say. She was pacing the floor of my apartment when I returned. The cats were ignoring her. While books say that cats are frightened of ghosts, mine had no problems with Olive, merely ignoring her. This was actually quite friendly for them considering they'd run away when most other people visited my apartment. Not that I had many visitors.

Perhaps they were just used to Olive.

"Well?" Olive demanded as I walked in. "What was going on? I heard you were held hostage. And in the garage of all places! I knew they shouldn't have built that. We could have used the extra space for storage for the restaurant or even a large walk-in freezer or refrigerator."

"We're going to add another camera there," I said. "I think that Nancy was hiding there for a few days. For some reason she thought I'd seen something about the embezzling she and Logan were doing."

"I heard," Olive said. "I was there when Suzanne

learned what was going on. To have you so close only to be harmed because it's not a place I can get to is rather distressing, if you don't mind my saying so."

"It was even worse being down there." I sighed and settled on the sofa. Chai had been on the arm of the sofa and moved a little when I sat. Latte was behind me and immediately stuck his front paws out to push against my head. I'm never certain if he does that because I'm encroaching on his space or because he wants to touch me.

"I would have told you what I found out. Bill saw a woman come out of the dojo that night and take the truck. He just remembered. Time is weird for him..."

"It is for us all," Olive interrupted.

"At any rate, I was going to go searching to see who she was and maybe try and find a photo so you could look out for her. But she was in the garage since she murdered her brother."

"It seems quite rude to murder one's brother. Although, Liliane temps me to familicide."

"By the way, your cousin is shopping for an attorney. It seemed her last one dropped the case but she's not happy about it."

"Really, you ought to do some research on my living family. Ask Ari to help you. Then I can figure out a way to drop a new bombshell on them and get Liliane off your back. She'll pay attention to whatever is most in front of her. Unfortunately, it seems that she came here and now this is in front of her. Or maybe she started reading and saw one of my books. Who knows?" Olive shook her head, looking up at the ceiling as if attempting to understand her cousin.

"I'm hopeful that most other attorneys will tell her the same thing as McDaniel did. The person Ari sent me to is quite a good attorney and apparently the first one to call seemed more than happy to go away after talking to the paralegal."

"That's good at least. But I'm sure it would be easier if there were something else to occupy her time."

Olive had settled a bit, but she still looked rather pensive.

"I can't believe that there was enough money in a vampire conference to make embezzling worthwhile."

"There were a lot of people here. And Logan barely paid for things. I guess he didn't pay any of the speakers and stopped paying for travel for a lot of them," I said. "He didn't get much. He'd have likely just gotten a slap on the wrist if Nancy hadn't started killing people. Now he's an accessory or whatever."

"People get themselves up into all kinds of odd situations," Olive said. "And it seems that your investigations get you carried along with them. I really ought to have modeled my character off of you. You do seem to have a nose for trouble."

"I'm sure Detective Granger would agree with you," I said.

Olive sniffed. "Only if she's smart."

I wondered if that meant I wasn't very smart.

"Still, I'm almost done with my second book. I'm even happier about this one than the last one. Hopefully, Liliane won't notice when it comes out or if she does, there'll be something more interesting for her to focus on. I'll have to give it some thought while we have Ari and you look into the people still living."

Olive popped out on that almost ominous note, leaving me alone with the cats.

My stomach growled a bit and I pushed myself up to make a bit of soup. I wasn't terribly hungry but I knew I ought to eat. The cats watched hopefully. They came running when I opened the can of soup and I had to disappoint them that I wasn't feeding them.

My back and side ached where I'd been kicked and a headache was throbbing. Fortunately, it was nothing that a good night's sleep wouldn't cure. I was told that I had only a minor concussion. While I shouldn't sleep too long unless someone was there to wake me, I could at least spend time at home.

It was far better than the hospital.

Eating my soup, I was incredibly grateful to have my little apartment, my cats, and my friends. While it'd been hard to get out of my shell and meet more people, I'd been quite pleased to see both Lyle and Suzanne at the hospital. Fortunately, neither of them were the sort to fuss, because I'd have hated that. But it was nice to know they cared enough to check up on me.

Finishing the soup, I looked at my two Siamese.

"And I always have you two, don't I?"

Both of them gave me a scratchy meow and then turned away to finish their interrupted naps.

I could appreciate the sentiment. Who needed someone getting all mushy and clingy when life was for living, or in their cases, life was for napping and bird watching and eating. There were worse ways to spend a day, I suppose.

About Bonnie Elizabeth

Bonnie Elizabeth writes in a variety of genres, including paranormal cozy mystery, paranormal women's fiction, contemporary fantasy, and gothic novels. Her shorts stories span most genres.

She has worked as a veterinary receptionist, library assistant, acupuncturist, and cemetery administrator before settling down to write. Her stories draw from this wide variety of experience and her often dark humor.

Currently she lives at home with her cats and her husband and is at work on her next novel or short story or whatever the heck the manuscript ends up being.

Stay in Touch

Also By Bonnie Elizabeth

The Haunted Hotel Series

The Ghost in Room 785

The Ghost in My Hotel

Jewel Midlife Magic Series

Bones of Connection

Dragons of Protection

Heart of Resurrection

Familiar Cafe Series

Unfamiliar Magic

Unfair Magic

Ash Jericho Series

An Inheritance to Die For

A Discovery to Die For

A Distraction to Die For